Zastrozzi

by Percy Shelley

Chapter I.

--That their God

May prove their foe, and with repenting hand

Abolish his own works--This would surpass

Common revenge.   .

--Paradise Lost.

Torn from the society of all he held dear on earth, the victim of secret enemies, and exiled from happiness, was the wretched Verezzi!

All was quiet; a pitchy darkness in volved the face of things, when, urged by fiercest revenge, placed himself at the door of the inn where, undisturbed, Verezzi slept.

Loudly he called the landlord. The landlord, to whom the bare name of was terrible, trembling obeyed the summons.

"Thou knowest Verezzi the Italian? he lodges here." "He does," answered the landlord.

"Him, then, have I devoted to destruction," exclaimed . "Let Ugo and Bernardo follow you to his apartment; I will be with you to prevent mischief."

Cautiously they ascended--successfully they executed their revengeful purpose, and bore the sleeping Verezzi to the place, where a chariot waited to convey the vindictive 's prey to the place of its destination.

Ugo and Bernardo lifted the still sleeping Verezzi into the chariot. Rapidly they travelled onwards for several hours. Verezzi was still wrapped in deep sleep, from which all the movements he had undergone had been insufficient to rouse him.

Zastrozzi and Ugo were masked, as was Bernardo, who acted as postition.

It was still dark, when they stopped at a small inn, on a remote and desolate heath; and waiting but to change horses, again advanced. At last day appeared--still the slumbers of Verezzi remained unbroken.

Ugo fearfully questioned as to the cause of his extraordinary sleep. Zastrozzi, who, however, was well acquainted with it, gloomily answered, "I know not."

Swiftly they travelled during the whole of the day, over which nature seemed to have drawn her most gloomy curtain.--They stopped occasionally at inns to change horses and obtain refreshments.

Night came on--they forsook the beaten track, and, entering an immense forest, made their way slowly through the rugged underwood.

At last they stopped--they lifted their victim from the chariot, and bore him to a cavern, which yawned in a dell close by.

Not long did the hapless victim of unmerited persecution enjoy an oblivion which deprived him of a knowledge of his horrible situation. He awoke--and overcome by excess of terror, started violently from the ruffians' arms.

They had now entered the cavern--Verezzi supported himself against a fragment of rock which jutted out.

"Resistance is useless," exclaimed ; "following us in submissive silence can alone procure the slightest mitigation of your punishment."

Verezzi followed as fast as his frame, weakened by unnatural sleep, and enfeebled by recent illness, would permit; yet, scarcely believing that he was awake, and not thoroughly convinced of the reality of the scene before him, he viewed every thing with that kind of inexplicable horror, which a terrible dream is wont to excite.

After winding down the rugged descent for some time, they arrived at an iron door, which at first sight appeared to be part of the rock itself. Every thing had till now been obscured by total darkness; and Verezzi, for the first time, saw the masked faces of his persecutors, which a torch brought by Bernardo rendered visible.

The massy door flew open.

The torches from without rendered the darkness which reigned within still more horrible; and Verezzi beheld the interior of this cavern as a place whence he was never again about to emerge--as his grave. Again he struggled with his persecutors, but his enfeebled frame was insufficient to support a conflict with the strong-nerved Ugo, and, subdued, he sank fainting into his arms.

His triumphant persecutor bore him into the damp cell, and chained him to the wall. An iron chain encircled his waist; his limbs, which not even a little straw kept from the rock, were fixed by immense staples to the flinty floor; and but one of his hands was left at liberty, to take the scanty pittance of bread and water which was daily allowed him.

Every thing was denied him but thought, which, by comparing the present with the past, was his greatest torment.

Ugo entered the cell every morning and evening, to bring coarse bread, and a pitcher of water, seldom, yet sometimes, accompanied by .

In vain did he implore mercy, pity, and even death: useless were all his enquiries concerning the cause of his barbarous imprisonment--a stern silence was maintained by his relentless gaoler.

Languishing in painful captivity, Verezzi passed days and nights seemingly countless, in the same monotonous uniformity of horror and despair. He scarcely now shuddered when the slimy lizard crossed his naked and motionless limbs. The large earth-worms, which twined themselves in his long and matted hair, almost ceased to excite sensations of horror.

Days and nights were undistinguishable from each other; and the period which he had passed there, though in reality but a few weeks, was lengthened by his perturbed imagination into many years. Sometimes he scarcely supposed that his torments were earthly, but that Ugo, whose countenance bespoke him a demon, was the fury who blasted his reviving hopes. His mysterious removal from the inn near Munich also confused his ideas, and he never could bring his thoughts to any conclusion on the subject which occupied them.

One evening, overcome by long watching, he sank to sleep, for almost the first time since his confinement, when he was aroused by a loud crash, which seemed to burst over the cavern. Attentively he listened--he even hoped, though hope was almost dead within his breast. Again he listened--again the same noise was repeated--it was but a violent thunderstorm which shook the elements above.

Convinced of the folly of hope, he addressed a prayer to his Creator--to Him who hears a suppliant from the bowels of the earth. His thoughts were elevated above terrestrial enjoyments--his sufferings sank into nothing on the comparison.

Whilst his thoughts were thus employed, a more violent crash shook the cavern. A scintillating flame darted from the cieling to the floor. Almost at the same instant the roof fell in.

A large fragment of the rock was laid athwart the cavern; one end being grooved into the solid wall, the other having almost forced open the massy iron door.

Verezzi was chained to a piece of rock which remained immoveable. The violence of the storm was past, but the hail descended rapidly, each stone of which wounded his naked limbs. Every flash of lightning, although now distant, dazzled his eyes, unaccustomed as they had been to the least ray of light.

The storm at last ceased, the pealing thunders died away in indistinct murmurs, and the lightning was too faint to be visible. Day appeared--no one had yet been to the cavern--Verezzi concluded that they either intended him to perish with hunger, or that some misfortune, by which they themselves had suffered, had occurred. In the most solemn manner, therefore, he now prepared himself for death, which he was fully convinced within himself was rapidly approaching.

His pitcher of water was broken by the falling fragments, and a small crust of bread was all that now remained of his scanty allowance of provisions.

A burning fever raged through his veins; and, delirious with despairing illness, he cast from him the crust which alone could now retard the rapid advances of death.

Oh! what ravages did the united efforts of disease and suffering make on the manly and handsome figure of Verezzi! His bones had almost started through his skin; his eyes were sunken and hollow; and his hair, matted with the damps, hung in strings upon his faded cheek. The day passed as had the morning-- death was every instant before his eyes--a lingering death by famine--he felt its approaches: night came, but with it brought no change. He was aroused by a noise against the iron door: it was the time when Ugo usually brought fresh provisions. The noise lessened, at last it totally ceased--with it ceased all hope of life in Verezzi's bosom. A cold tremor pervaded his limbs--his eyes but faintly presented to his imagination the ruined cavern--he sank, as far as the chain which encircled his waist would permit him, upon the flinty pavement; and, in the crisis of the fever which then occurred, his youth and good constitution prevailed.

Chapter II.

In the mean time Ugo, who had received orders from not to allow Verezzi to die, came at the accustomed hour to bring provisions, but finding that, in the last night's storm, the rock had been struck by lightning, concluded that Verezzi had lost his life amid the ruins, and he went with this news to Zastrozzi.--Zastrozzi, who, for inexplicable reasons, wished not Verezzi's death, sent Ugo and Bernardo to search for him.

After a long scrutiny, they discovered their hapless victim. He was chained to the rock where they had left him, but in that exhausted condition, which want of food, and a violent fever, had reduced him to.

They unchained him, and lifting him into a chariot, after four hours rapid travelling, brought the insensible Verezzi to a cottage, inhabited by an old woman alone. The cottage stood on an immense heath, lonely, desolate, and remote from other human habitation.

Zastrozzi awaited their arrival with impatience: eagerly he flew to meet them, and, with a demoniac smile, surveyed the agonised features of his prey, who lay insensible and stretched on the shoulders of Ugo.

"His life must not be lost," exclaimed ; "I have need of it. Tell Bianca, therefore, to prepare a bed."

Ugo obeyed, and Bernardo followed, bearing the emaciated Verezzi. A physician was sent for, who declared, that the crisis of the fever which had attacked him being past, proper care might reinstate him; but that the disorder having attacked his brain, a tranquillity of mind was absolutely necessary for his recovery.

, to whom the life, though not the happiness of Verezzi was requisite, saw that his too eager desire for revenge had carried him beyond his point. He saw that some deception was requisite; he accordingly instructed the old woman to inform him, when he recovered, that he was placed in this situation, because the physicians had asserted that the air of this country was necessary for a recovery from a brain fever which had attacked him.

It was long before Verezzi recovered--long did he languish in torpid insensibility, during which his soul seemed to have winged its way to happier regions.

At last, however, he recovered, and the first use he made of his senses was to inquire where he was.

The old woman told him the story, which she had been instructed in by .

"Who ordered me then to be chained in that desolate and dark cavern," inquired Verezzi, "where I have been for many years, and suffered most insupportable torments?"

"Lord bless me!" said the old woman: "why, baron, how strangely you talk! I begin to fear you will again lose your senses, at the very time when you ought to be thanking God for suffering them to return to you. What can you mean by being chained in a cavern? I declare I am frightened at the very thought: pray do compose yourself."

Verezzi was much perplexed by the old woman's assertions. That Julia should send him to a mean cottage, and desert him, was impossible.

The old woman's relation seemed so well connected, and told with such an air of characteristic simplicity, that he could not disbelieve her.

But to doubt the evidence of his own senses, and the strong proofs of his imprisonment, which the deep marks of the chains had left till now, was impossible.

Had not those marks still remained, he would have conceived the horrible events which had led him thither to have been but the dreams of his perturbed imagination. He, however, thought it better to yield, since, as Ugo and Bernardo attended him in the short walks he was able to take, an escape was impossible, and its attempt would but make his situation more unpleasant.

He often expressed a wish to write to Julia, but the old woman said she had orders neither to permit him to write nor receive letters--on pretence of not agitating his mind; and to avoid the consequences of despair, knives were denied him.

As Verezzi recovered, and his mind obtained that firm tone which it was wont to possess, he perceived that it was but a device of his enemies that detained him at the cottage, and his whole thoughts were now bent upon the means for effecting his escape.

It was late one evening, when, tempted by the peculiar beauty of the weather, Verezzi wandered beyond the usual limits, attended by Ugo and Bernardo, who narrowly watched his every movement. Immersed in thought, he wandered onwards, till he came to a woody eminence, whose beauty tempted him to rest a little, in a seat carved in the side of an ancient oak. Forgetful of his unhappy and dependent situation, he sat there some time, until Ugo told him that it was time to return.

In their absence, had arrived at the cottage. He had impatiently enquired for Verezzi.

"It is the baron's custom to walk every evening," said Bianca; "I soon expect him to return."

Verezzi at last arrived.

Not knowing as he entered, he started back, overcome by the likeness he bore to one of the men he had seen in the cavern.

He was now convinced that all the sufferings which he had undergone in that horrible abode of misery were not imaginary, and that he was at this instant in the power of his bitterest enemy.

's eyes were fixed on him with an expression too manifest to be misunderstood; and with an air in which he struggled to disguise the natural malevolence of his heart, he said, that he hoped Verezzi's health had not suffered from the evening air.

Enraged beyond measure at this hypocrisy, from a man whom he now no longer doubted to be the cause of all his misfortunes, he could not forbear inquiring for what purpose he had conveyed him hither, and told him instantly to release him.

's cheeks turned pale with passion, his lips quivered, his eyes darted revengeful glances, as thus he spoke:--

"Retire to your chamber, young fool, which is the fittest place for you to reflect on, and repent of, the insolence shown to one so much your superior."

"I fear nothing," interrupted Verezzi, "from your vain threats and empty denunciations of vengeance: justice, Heaven! is on my side, and I must eventually triumph."

What can be a greater proof of the superiority of virtue, than that the terrible, the dauntless trembled! for he did tremble; and, conquered by the emotions of the moment, paced the circumscribed apartment with unequal steps. For an instant he shrunk within himself: he thought of his past life, and his awakened conscience reflected images of horror. But again revenge drowned the voice of virtue--again passion obscured the light of reason, and his steeled soul persisted in its scheme.

Whilst he still thought, Ugo entered. , smothering his stinging conscience, told Ugo to follow him to the heath.--Ugo obeyed.

Chapter III.

Zastrozzi and Ugo proceeded along the heath, on the skirts of which stood the cottage. Verezzi leaned against the casement, when a low voice, which floated in indistinct murmurs on the silence of the evening, reached his ear.--He listened attentively. He looked into the darkness, and saw the towering form of Zastrozzi, and Ugo, whose awkward, ruffian-like gait, could never be mistaken. He could not hear their discourse, except a few detached words which reached his ears. They seemed to be denunciations of anger; a low tone afterwards succeeded, and it appeared as if a dispute, which had arisen between them, was settled: their voices at last died away in distance.

Bernardo now left the room: Bianca entered; but Verezzi plainly heard Bernardo lingering at the door.

The old woman continued sitting in silence at a remote corner of the chamber. It was Verezzi's hour for supper:--he desired Bianca to bring it. She obeyed, and brought some dried raisins in a plate. He was surprised to see a knife was likewise brought; an indulgence he imputed to the inadvertency of the old woman.--A thought started across his mind--it was now time to escape.

He seized the knife--he looked expressively at the old woman--she trembled. He advanced from the casement to the door: he called for Bernardo--Bernardo entered, and Verezzi, lifting his arm high, aimed the knife at the villain's heart.--Bernardo started aside, and the knife was fixed firmly in the doorcase. Verezzi attempted by one effort to extricate it. The effort was vain. Bianca, as fast as her tottering limbs could carry her, hastened through the opposite door, calling loudly for .

Verezzi attempted to rush through the open door, but Bernardo opposed himself to it. A long and violent contest ensued, and Bernardo's superior strength was on the point of overcoming Verezzi, when the latter, by a dexterous blow, precipitated him down the steep and narrow staircase.

Not waiting to see the event of his victory, he rushed through the opposite door, and meeting with no opposition, ran swiftly across the heath.

The moon, in tranquil majesty, hung high in air, and showed the immense extent of the plain before him. He continued rapidly advancing, and the cottage was soon out of sight. He thought that he heard 's voice in every gale. Turning round, he thought Zastrozzi's eye glanced over his shoulder.--But even had Bianca taken the right road, and found Zastrozzi, Verezzi's speed would have mocked pursuit.

He ran several miles, still the dreary extent of the heath was before him: no cottage yet appeared where he might take shelter. He cast himself, for an instant, on the bank of a rivulet, which stole slowly across the heath. The moonbeam played upon its surface--he started at his own reflected image--he thought that voices were wafted on the western gale, and, nerved anew, pursued his course across the plain.

The moon had gained the zenith before Verezzi rested again. Two pine trees, of extraordinary size, stood on a small eminence: he climbed one, and found a convenient seat in its immense branches.

Fatigued, he sank to sleep.

Two hours he lay hushed in oblivion, when he was awakened by a noise. It is but the hooting of the night-raven, thought he.

Day had not yet appeared, but faint streaks in the east presaged the coming morn. Verezzi heard the clattering of hoofs--What was his horror to see that , Bernardo, and Ugo, were the horsemen! Overcome by terror, he clung to the rugged branch. His persecutors advanced to the spot--they stopped under the tree wherein he was.

"Eternal curses," exclaimed , "upon Verezzi! I swear never to rest until I find him, and then I will accomplish the purpose of my soul.--But come, Ugo, Bernardo, let us proceed."

"Signor," said Ugo, "let us the rather stop here to refresh ourselves and our horses. You, perhaps, will not make this pine your couch, but I will get up, for I think I spy an excellent bed above there."

"No, no," answered ; "did not I resolve never to rest until I had found Verezzi? Mount, villain, or die."

Ugo sullenly obeyed. They galloped off, and were quickly out of sight.

Verezzi returned thanks to Heaven for his escape; for he thought that Ugo's eye, as the villain pointed to the branch where he reposed, met his.

It was now morning. Verezzi surveyed the heath, and thought he saw buildings at a distance. Could he gain a town or city, he might defy 's power.

He descended the pine-tree, and advanced as quickly as he could towards the distant buildings. He proceeded across the heath for half an hour, and perceived that, at last, he had arrived at its termination.

The country assumed a new aspect, and the number of cottages and villas showed him that he was in the neighbourhood of some city. A large road which he now entered confirmed his opinion. He saw two peasants, and asked them where the road led.--"To Passau," was the answer.

It was yet very early in the morning, when he walked through the principal street of Passau. He felt very faint with his recent and unusual exertions; and, overcome by languor, sank on some lofty stone steps, which led to a magnificent mansion, and resting his head on his arm, soon fell asleep.

He had been there nearly an hour, when he was awakened by an old woman. She had a basket on her arm, in which were flowers, which it was her custom to bring to Passau every market-day. Hardly knowing where he was, he answered the old woman's inquiries in a vague and unsatisfactory manner. By degrees, however, they became better acquainted; and as Verezzi had no money, nor any means of procuring it, he accepted of an offer which Claudine (for that was the old woman's name) made him, to work for her, and share her cottage, which, together with a little garden, was all she could call her own. Claudine quickly disposed of her flowers, and accompanied by Verezzi, soon arrived at a little cottage near Passau. It was situated on a pleasant and cultivated spot; at the foot of a small eminence, on which it was situated, flowed the majestic Danube, and on the opposite side was a forest belonging to the Baron of Schwepper, whose vassal Claudine was.

Her little cottage was kept extremely neat; and, by the charity of the Baron, wanted none of those little comforts which old age requires.

Verezzi thought that, in so retired a spot, he might at least pass his time tranquilly, and elude .

"What induced you," said he to Claudine, as in the evening they sat before the cottage-door, "what induced you to make that offer this morning to me?"

"Ah!" said the old woman, "it was but last week that I lost my dear son, who was every thing to me: he died by a fever which he caught by his too great exertions in obtaining a livelihood for me; and I came to the market yesterday, for the first time since my son's death, hoping to find some peasant who would fill his place, when chance threw you in my way.

"I had hoped that he would have outlived me, as I am quickly hastening to the grave, to which I look forward as to the coming of a friend, who would relieve me from those cares which, alas! but increase with my years."

Verezzi's heart was touched with compassion for the forlorn situation of

Claudine. He tenderly told her that he would not forsake her; but if any opportunity occurred for ameliorating her situation, she should no longer continue in poverty.

Chapter IV.

But let us return to .--He had walked with Ugo on the heath, and had returned late. He was surprised to see no light in the cottage. He advanced to the door-- he rapped violently--no one answered. "Very strange!" exclaimed Zastrozzi, as he burst open the door with his foot. He entered the cottage--no one was there: he searched it, and at last saw Bernardo lying, seemingly lifeless, at the foot of the staircase. Zastrozzi advanced to him, and lifted him from the ground: he had been but in a trance, and immediately recovered.

As soon as his astonishment was dissipated, he told what had happened.

"What!" exclaimed , interrupting him, "Verezzi escaped! Hell and furies! Villain, you deserve instant death; but thy life is at present necessary to me. Arise, go instantly to Rosenheim, and bring three of my horses from the inn there--make haste! begone!"

Bernardo trembling arose, and obeying 's commands, crossed the heath quickly towards Rosenheim, a village about half a league distant on the north.

Whilst he was gone, , agitated by contending passions, knew scarcely what to do. With hurried strides he paced the cottage. He sometimes spoke lowly to himself. The feelings of his soul flashed from his eyes--his frown was terrible.

"Would I had his heart reeking on my dagger, Signor!" said Ugo. "Kill him when you catch him, which you soon will, I am sure."

"Ugo," said , "you are my friend; you advise me well.--But, no! he must not die.--Ah! by what horrible fetters am I chained--fool that I was--Ugo! he shall die--die by the most hellish torments. I give myself up to fate:--I will taste revenge; for revenge is sweeter than life: and even were I to die with him, and, as the punishment of my crime, be instantly plunged into eternal torments, I should taste superior joy in recollecting the sweet moment of his destruction. O! would that destruction could be eternal!"

The clattering of hoofs was heard, and was now interrupted by the arrival of Bernardo--they instantly mounted, and the high-spirited steeds bore them swiftly across the heath.

Rapidly, for some time, were and his companions borne across the plain. They took the same road as Verezzi had. They passed the pines where he reposed. They hurried on.

The fainting horses were scarce able to bear their guilty burthens. No one had spoken since they had left the clustered pines.

Bernardo's horse, overcome by excessive fatigue, sank on the ground; that of scarce appeared in better condition.--They stopped.

"What!" exclaimed , "must we give up the search! Ah! I am afraid we must; our horses can proceed no farther--curse on the horses.

"But let us proceed on foot--Verezzi shall not escape me--nothing shall now retard the completion of my just revenge."

As he thus spoke, 's eye gleamed with impatient revenge; and, with rapid steps, he advanced towards the south of the heath.

Day-light at length appeared; still were the villain's efforts to find Verezzi inefficient. Hunger, thirst, and fatigue, conspired to make them relinquish the pursuit--they lay at intervals upon the stony soil.

"This is but an uncomfortable couch, Signor," muttered Ugo.

, whose whole thoughts were centred in revenge, heeded him not, but nerved anew by impatient vengeance, he started from the bosom of the earth, and muttering curses upon the innocent object of his hatred, proceeded onwards. The day passed as had the morning and preceding night. Their hunger was scantily allayed by the wild berries which grew amid the heathy shrubs; and their thirst but increased by the brackish pools of water which alone they met with. They perceived a wood at some distance. "That is a likely place for Verezzi to have retired to, for the day is hot, and he must want repose as well as ourselves," said Bernardo. "True," replied Zastrozzi, as he advanced towards it. They quickly arrived at its borders: it was not a wood, but an immense forest, which stretched southward as far as Schauffhausen. They advanced into it.

The tall trees rising above their heads warded off the meridian sun; the mossy banks beneath invited repose: but , little recking a scene so fair, hastily scrutinised every recess which might afford an asylum to Verezzi.

Useless were all his researches--fruitless his endeavours: still, however, though faint with hunger, and weary with exertion, he nearly sank upon the turf. His mind was superior to corporeal toil; for that, nerved by revenge, was indefatigable.

Ugo and Bernardo, overcome by the extreme fatigue which they had undergone, and strong as the assassins were, fell fainting on the earth.

The sun began to decline; at last it sank beneath the western mountain, and the forest-tops were tinged by its departing ray. The shades of night rapidly thickened.

Zastrozzi sat a while upon the decayed trunk of a scathed oak.

The sky was serene; the blue ether was spangled with countless myriads of stars: the tops of the lofty forest-trees waved mournfully in the evening wind; and the moon-beam penetrating at intervals, as they moved, through the matted branches, threw dubious shades upon the dark underwood beneath.

Ugo and Bernardo, conquered by irresistible torpor, sank to rest upon the dewy turf.

A scene so fair--a scene so congenial to those who can reflect upon their past lives with pleasure, and anticipate the future with the enthusiasm of innocence, ill accorded with the ferocious soul of , which at one time agitated by revenge, at another by agonising remorse, or contending passions, could derive no pleasure from the past--anticipate no happiness in futurity.

Zastrozzi sat for some time immersed in heart-rending contemplations; but though conscience for a while reflected his past life in images of horror, again was his heart steeled by fiercest vengeance; and, aroused by images of insatiate revenge, he hastily arose, and, waking Ugo and Bernardo, pursued his course.

The night was calm and serene--not a cloud obscured the azure brilliancy of the spangled concave above--not a wind ruffled the tranquillity of the atmosphere below.

, Ugo, and Bernardo, advanced into the forest. They had tasted no food, save the wild berries of the wood, for some time, and were anxious to arrive at some cottage, where they might procure refreshments. For some time the deep silence which reigned was uninterrupted.

"What is that?" exclaimed , as he beheld a large and magnificent building, whose battlements rose above the lofty trees. It was built in the Gothic style of architecture, and appeared to be inhabited.

The building reared its pointed casements loftily to the sky: their treillaged ornaments were silvered by the clear moon-light, to which the dark shades of the arches beneath formed a striking contrast. A large portico jutted out: they advanced towards it, and attempted to open the door.

An open window on one side of the casement arrested 's attention. "Let us enter that," said he.--They entered. It was a large saloon, with many windows. Every thing within was arranged with princely magnificence.--Four ancient and immense sofas in the apartment invited repose.

Near one of the windows stood a table, with an escrutoire on it; a paper lay on the ground near it.

, as he passed, heedlessly took up the paper. He advanced nearer to the window, thinking his senses had deceived him when he read, "La Contessa di Laurentini;" but they had not done so, for La Contessa di Laurentini still continued on the paper. He hastily opened it; and the letter, though of no importance, convinced him that this must have been the place to which Matilda said that she had removed.

Ugo and Bernardo lay sleeping on the sofas. , leaving them as they were, opened an opposite door--it led into a vaulted hall--a large flight of stairs rose from the opposite side--he ascended them--He advanced along a lengthened corridor--a female in white robes stood at the other end--a lamp burnt near her on the balustrade. She was in a reclining attitude, and had not observed his approach. Zastrozzi recognised her for Matilda. He approached her, and beholding Zastrozzi before her, she started back with surprise. For a while she gazed on him in silence, and at last exclaimed, "Zastrozzi! ah! are we revenged on Julia? am I happy? Answer me quickly. Well by your silence do I perceive that our plans have been put into execution. Excellent Zastrozzi! accept my most fervent thanks, my eternal gratitude."

"Matilda!" returned , "would I could say that we were happy! but, alas! it is but misery and disappointment that causes this my so unexpected visit. I know nothing of the Marchesa di Strobazzo--less of Verezzi. I fear that I must wait till age has unstrung my now so fervent energies; and when time has damped your passion, perhaps you may gain Verezzi's love. Julia is returned to Italy--is even now in Naples; and, secure in the immensity of her possessions, laughs at our trifling vengeance. But it shall not be always thus," continued Zastrozzi, his eyes sparkling with inexpressible brilliancy; "I will accomplish my purpose; and, Matilda, thine shall likewise be effected. But, come, I have not tasted food for these two days."

"Oh! supper is prepared below," said Matilda. Seated at the supper-table, the conversation, enlivened by wine, took an animated turn. After some subjects, irrelevant to this history, being discussed, Matilda said, "Ha! but I forgot to tell you, that I have done some good: I have secured that diabolical Paulo, Julia's servant, who was of great service to her, and, by penetrating our schemes, might have even discomfited our grand design. I have lodged him in the lowest cavern of those dungeons which are under this building--will you go and see him?" answered in the affirmative, and seizing a lamp which burnt in a recess of the apartment, followed Matilda.

The rays of the lamp but partially dissipated the darkness as they advanced through the antiquated passages. They arrived at a door: Matilda opened it, and they quickly crossed a grass-grown court-yard.

The grass which grew on the lofty battlements waved mournfully in the rising blast, as Matilda and entered a dark and narrow casement.--Cautiously they descended the slippery and precipitous steps. The lamp, obscured by the vapours, burnt dimly as they advanced. They arrived at the foot of the staircase. "Zastrozzi!" exclaimed Matilda. Zastrozzi turned quickly, and, perceiving a door, obeyed Matilda's directions.

On some straw, chained to the wall, lay Paulo.

"O pity! stranger, pity!" exclaimed the miserable Paulo.

No answer, save a smile of most expressive scorn, was given by . They again ascended the narrow staircase, and, passing the court-yard, arrived at the supper-room.

"But," said , again taking his seat, "what use is that fellow Paulo in the dungeon? why do you keep him there?"

"Oh!" answered Matilda, "I know not; but if you wish"--

She paused, but her eye expressively filled up the sentence.

Zastrozzi poured out an overflowing goblet of wine. He summoned Ugo and Bernardo--"Take that," said Matilda, presenting them a key--One of the villains took it, and in a few moments returned with the hapless Paulo.

"Paulo!" exclaimed loudly, "I have prevailed on La Contessa to restore your freedom: here," added he, "take this; I pledge you to your future happiness."

Paulo bowed low--he drank the poisoned potion to the dregs, and, overcome by sudden and irresistible faintness, fell at 's feet. Sudden convulsions shook his frame, his lips trembled, his eyes rolled horribly, and, uttering an agonised and lengthened groan, he expired.

"Ugo! Bernardo! take that body and bury it immediately," cried . "There, Matilda, by such means must Julia die: you see, that the poisons which I possess are quick in their effect."

A pause ensued, during which the eyes of and Matilda spoke volumes to each guilty soul.

The silence was interrupted by Matilda. Not shocked at the dreadful outrage which had been committed, she told to come out into the forest, for that she had something for his private ear.

"Matilda," said , as they advanced along the forest, "I must not stay here, and waste moments in inactivity, which might be more usefully employed: I must quit you to-morrow--I must destroy Julia."

"," returned Matilda, "I am so far from wishing you to spend your time here in ignoble listlessness, that I will myself join your search. You shall to Italy-- to Naples--watch Julia's every movement, attend her every step, and in the guise of a friend destroy her: but beware, whilst you assume the softness of the dove, to forget not the cunning of the serpent. On you I depend for destroying her, my own exertions shall find Verezzi; I myself will gain his love--Julia must die, and expiate the crime of daring to rival me, with her hated blood."

Whilst thus they conversed, whilst they planned these horrid schemes of destruction, the night wore away.

The moon-beam darting her oblique rays from under volumes of louring vapour, threatened an approaching storm. The lurid sky was tinged with a yellowish lustre--the forest-tops rustled in the rising tempest--big drops fell--a flash of lightning, and, instantly after, a peal of bursting thunder, struck with sudden terror the bosom of Matilda. She, however, immediately overcame it, and regarding the battling element with indifference, continued her discourse with .

They wore out the night in many visionary plans for the future, and now and then a gleam of remorse assailed Matilda's heart. Heedless of the storm, they had remained in the forest late. Flushed with wickedness, they at last sought their respective couches, but sleep forsook their pillow.

In all the luxuriance of extravagant fancy, Matilda portrayed the symmetrical form, the expressive countenance, of Verezzi; whilst , who played a double part, anticipated, with ferocious exultation, the torments which he she loved was eventually fated to endure, and changed his plan, for a sublimer mode of vengeance was opened to his view.

Matilda passed a night of restlessness and agitation: her mind was harassed by contending passions, and her whole soul wound up to deeds of horror and wickedness. 's countenance, as she met him in the breakfast-parlour, wore a settled expression of determined revenge--"I almost shudder," exclaimed

Matilda, "at the sea of wickedness on which I am about to embark! But still, Verezzi--ah! for him would I even lose my hopes of eternal happiness. In the sweet idea of calling him mine, no scrupulous delicacy, no mistaken superstitious fear, shall prevent me from deserving him by daring acts--No! I am resolved," continued Matilda, as, recollecting his graceful form, her soul was assailed by tenfold love--

"And I am likewise resolved," said ; "I am resolved on revenge--my revenge shall be gratified. Julia shall die, and Verezzi--"

Zastrozzi paused; his eye gleamed with a peculiar expression, and Matilda thought he meant more than he had said--she raised her eyes--they encountered his.

The guilt-bronzed cheek of was tinged with a momentary blush, but it quickly passed away, and his countenance recovered its wonted firm and determined expression.

"!" exclaimed Matilda,--"should you be false--should you seek to deceive me--But, no, it is impossible.--Pardon, my friend--I meant not what I said--my thoughts are crazed--"

"Tis well," said , haughtily.

"But you forgive my momentary, unmeaning doubt?" said Matilda, and fixed her unmeaning eyes on his countenance.

"It is not for us to dwell on vain, unmeaning expressions, which the soul dictates not," returned ; "and I sue for pardon from you, for having, by ambiguous expressions, caused the least agitation: but, believe me, Matilda, we will not forsake each other; your cause is mine; distrust between us is foolish.--But, farewell for the present; I must order Bernardo to go to Passau, to purchase horses."

The day passed on; each waited with impatience for the arrival of Bernardo.--"Farewell, Matilda," exclaimed , as he mounted the horses which Bernardo brought; and, taking the route of Italy, galloped off.

Chapter V.

Her whole soul wrapped up in one idea, the guilty Matilda threw herself into a chariot which waited at the door, and ordered the equipage to proceed towards Passau.

Left to indulge reflection in solitude, her mind recurred to the object nearest her heart--to Verezzi.

Her bosom was scorched by an ardent and unquenchable fire; and while she thought of him, she even shuddered at the intenseness of her own sensations.

"He shall love me--he shall be mine--mine for ever," mentally ejaculated Matilda.

The streets of Passau echoed to La Contessa di Laurentini's equipage, before, roused from her reverie, she found herself at the place of destination; and she was seated in her hotel in that city, before she had well arranged her unsettled ideas. She summoned Ferdinand, a trusty servant, to whom she confided every thing.--"Ferdinand," said she, "you have many claims on my gratitude: I have never had cause to reproach you with infidelity in executing my purposes--add another debt to that which I already owe you: find Il Conte Verezzi within three days, and you are my best friend." Ferdinand bowed, and prepared to execute her commands. Two days passed, during which Matilda failed not to make every personal inquiry, even in the suburbs of Passau.

Alternately depressed by fear, and revived by hope, for three days was Matilda's mind in a state of disturbance and fluctuation. The evening of the third day, of the day on which Ferdinand was to return, arrived. Matilda's mind, wound up to the extreme of impatience, was the scene of conflicting passions.-

-She paced the room rapidly.

A servant entered, and announced supper.

"Is Ferdinand returned?" hastily inquired Matilda.

The domestic answered in the negative.--She sighed deeply, and struck her forehead.

Footsteps were heard in the antichamber without.

"There is Ferdinand!" exclaimed Matilda, exultingly, as he entered--"Well, well! have you found Verezzi? Ah! speak quickly! ease me of this horrible suspense."

"Signora!" said Ferdinand, "it grieves me much to be obliged to declare, that all my endeavours have been inefficient to find Il Conte Verezzi--."

"Oh, madness! madness!" exclaimed Matilda; "is it for this that I have plunged into the dark abyss of crime?--is it for this that I have despised the delicacy of my sex, and, braving consequences, have offered my love to one who despises me--who shuns me, as does the barbarous Verezzi? But if he is in Passau--if he is in the environs of the city, I will find him."

Thus saying, despising the remonstrances of her domestics, casting off all sense of decorum, she rushed into the streets of Passau. A gloomy silence reigned through the streets of the city; it was past midnight, and every inhabitant seemed to be sunk in sleep--sleep which Matilda was almost a stranger to. Her white robes floated on the night air--her shadowy and dishevelled hair flew over her form, which, as she passed the bridge, seemed to strike the boatmen below with the idea of some supernatural and ethereal form.

She hastily crossed the bridge--she entered the fields on the right--the

Danube, whose placid stream was scarcely agitated by the wind, reflected her symmetrical form, as, scarcely knowing what direction she pursued, Matilda hastened along its banks. Sudden horror, resistless despair, seized her brain, maddened as it was by hopeless love.

"What have I to do in this world, my fairest prospect blighted, my fondest hope rendered futile?" exclaimed the frantic Matilda, as, wound up to the highest pitch of desperation, she attempted to plunge herself into the river.

But life fled; for Matilda, caught by a stranger's arm, was prevented from the desperate act.

Overcome by horror, she fainted.

Some time did she lie in a state of torpid insensibility, till the stranger, filling his cap with water from the river, and sprinkling her pallid countenance with it, recalled to life the miserable Matilda.

What was her surprise, what was her mingled emotion of rapture and doubt, when the moon-beam disclosed to her view the countenance of Verezzi, as in anxious solicitude he bent over her elegantly-proportioned form!

"By what chance," exclaimed the surprised Verezzi, "do I see here La Contessa di Laurentini? did not I leave you at your Italian castella? I had hoped you would have ceased to persecute me, when I told you that I was irrevocably another's."

"Oh, Verezzi!" exclaimed Matilda, casting herself at his feet, "I adore you to madness--I love you to distraction. If you have one spark of compassion, let me not sue in vain--reject not one who feels it impossible to overcome the fatal, resistless passion which consumes her."

"Rise, Signora," returned Verezzi--"rise; this discourse is improper--it is not suiting the dignity of your rank, or the delicacy of your sex: but suffer me to conduct you to yon cottage, where, perhaps, you may deign to refresh yourself, or pass the night."

The moon-beams played upon the tranquil waters of the Danube, as Verezzi silently conducted the beautiful Matilda to the humble dwelling where he resided.

Claudine waited at the door, and had begun to fear that some mischance had befallen Verezzi, as, when he arrived at the cottage-door, it was long past his usual hour of return.

It was his custom, during those hours when the twilight of evening cools the air, to wander through the adjacent rich scenery, though he seldom prolonged his walks till midnight.

He supported the fainting form of Matilda as he advanced towards Claudine. The old woman's eyes had lately failed her, from extreme age; and it was not until Verezzi called to her that she saw him, accompanied by La Contessa di Laurentini.

"Claudine," said Verezzi, "I have another claim upon your kindness: this lady, who has wandered beyond her knowledge, will honour our cottage so far as to pass the night here. If you would prepare the pallet which I usually occupy for her, I will repose this evening on the turf, and will now get supper ready. Signora," continued he, addressing Matilda, "some wine would, I think, refresh your spirits; permit me to fill you a glass of wine."

Matilda silently accepted his offer--their eyes met--those of Matilda were sparkling and full of meaning.

"Verezzi!" exclaimed Matilda, "I arrived but four days since at Passau--I have eagerly inquired for you--oh! how eagerly!--Will you accompany me to-morrow to Passau?"

"Yes," said Verezzi, hesitatingly.

Claudine soon joined them. Matilda exulted in the success of her schemes, and Claudine being present, the conversation took a general turn. The lateness of the hour, at last, warned them to separate.

Verezzi, left to solitude and his own reflections, threw himself on the turf, which extended to the Danube below.--Ideas of the most gloomy nature took possession of his soul; and, in the event of the evening, he saw the foundation of the most bitter misfortunes.

He could not love Matilda; and though he never had seen her but in the most amiable light, he found it impossible to feel any sentiment towards her, save cold esteem. Never had he beheld those dark shades in her character, which, if developed, could excite nothing but horror and detestation: he regarded her as a woman of strong passions, who, having resisted them to the utmost of her power, was at last borne away in the current--whose brilliant virtues one fault had obscured--as such he pitied her: but still could he not help observing a comparison between her and Julia, whose feminine delicacy shrunk from the slightest suspicion, even of indecorum. Her fragile form, her mild heavenly countenance, was contrasted with all the partiality of love, to the scintillating eye, the commanding countenance, the bold expressive gaze, of Matilda.

He must accompany her on the morrow to Passau.--During their walk, he determined to observe a strict silence; or, at all events, not to hazard one equivocal expression, which might be construed into what it was not meant for.

The night passed away--morning came, and the tops of the far-seen mountains were gilded by the rising sun.

Exulting in the success of her schemes, and scarcely able to disguise the vivid feelings of her heart, the wily Matilda, as early she descended to the narrow parlour, where Claudine had prepared a simple breakfast, affected a gloom she was far from feeling.

An unequivocal expression of innocent and mild tenderness marked her manner towards Verezzi: her eyes were cast on the ground, and her every movement spoke meekness and sensibility.

At last, breakfast being finished, the time arrived when Matilda, accompanied by Verezzi, pursued the course of the river, to retrace her footsteps to Passau. A gloomy silence for some time prevailed--at last Matilda spoke.

"Unkind Verezzi! is it thus that you will ever slight me? is it for this that I have laid aside the delicacy of my sex, and owned to you a passion which was but too violent to be concealed?--Ah! at least pity me! I love you: oh! I adore you to madness!"

She paused--the peculiar expression which beamed in her dark eye, told the tumultuous wishes of her bosom.

"Distress not yourself and me, Signora," said Verezzi, "by these unavailing protestations. Is it for you--is it for Matilda," continued he, his countenance assuming a smile of bitterest scorn, "to talk of love to the lover of Julia?"

Rapid tears coursed down Matilda's cheek. She sighed--the sigh seemed to rend her inmost bosom.

So unexpected a reply conquered Verezzi. He had been prepared for reproaches, but his feelings could not withstand Matilda's tears.

"Ah! forgive me, Signora," exclaimed Verezzi, "if my brain, crazed by disappointments, dictated words which my heart intended not."

"Oh!" replied Matilda, "it is I who am wrong: led on by the violence of my passion, I have uttered words, the bare recollection of which fills me with horror. Oh! forgive, forgive an unhappy woman, whose only fault is loving you too well."

As thus she spoke, they entered the crowded streets of Passau, and, proceeding rapidly onwards, soon arrived at La Contessa di Laurentini's hotel.

Chapter VI.

The character of Matilda has been already so far revealed, as to render it unnecessary to expatiate upon it farther. Suffice it to say, that her syren illusions, and well-timed blandishments, obtained so great a power over the imagination of Verezzi, that his resolution to return to Claudine's cottage before sun-set became every instant fainter and fainter.

"And will you thus leave me?" exclaimed Matilda, in accents of the bitterest anguish, as Verezzi prepared to depart--"will you thus leave unnoticed, her who, for your sake alone, casting aside the pride of high birth, has wandered, unknown, through foreign climes? Oh! if I have (led away by love for you) outstepped the bounds of modesty, let me not, oh! let me not be injured by others with impunity. Stay, I entreat thee, Verezzi, if yet one spark of compassion lingers in your breast--stay and defend me from those who vainly seek one who is irrevocably thine."

With words such as these did the wily Matilda work upon the generous passions of Verezzi. Emotions of pity, of compassion, for one whose only fault he supposed to be love for him, conquered Verezzi's softened soul.

"Oh! Matilda," said he, "though I cannot love thee--though my soul is irrevocably another's--yet, believe me, I esteem, I admire thee; and it grieves me that a heart, fraught with so many and so brilliant virtues, has fixed itself on one who is incapable of appreciating its value."

The time passed away, and each returning sun beheld Verezzi still at Passau-- still under Matilda's proof. That softness, that melting tenderness, which she knew so well how to assume, began to convince Verezzi of the injustice of the involuntary hatred which had filled his soul towards her. Her conversation was fraught with sense and elegant ideas. She played to him in the cool of the evening; and often, after sun-set, they rambled together into the rich scenery and luxuriant meadows which are washed by the Danube.

Claudine was not forgotten: indeed, Matilda first recollected her, and, by placing her in an independent situation, added a new claim to the gratitude of Verezzi.

In this manner three weeks passed away. Every day did Matilda practise new arts, employ new blandishments, to detain under her roof the fascinated Verezzi.

The most select parties in Passau, flitted in varied movements to exquisite harmony, when Matilda perceived Verezzi's spirits to be ruffled by recollection.

When he seemed to prefer solitude, a moonlight walk by the Danube was proposed by Matilda; or, with skilful fingers, she drew from her harp sounds of the most heart-touching, most enchanting melody. Her behaviour towards him was soft, tender, and quiet, and might rather have characterised the mild, serene love of a friend or sister, than the ardent, unquenchable fire, which burnt, though concealed, within Matilda's bosom.

It was one calm evening that Matilda and Verezzi sat in a back saloon, which overlooked the gliding Danube. Verezzi was listening, with all the enthusiasm of silent rapture, to a favourite soft air which Matilda sang, when a loud rap at the hall door startled them. A domestic entered, and told Matilda that a stranger, on particular business, waited to speak with her.

"Oh!" exclaimed Matilda, "I cannot attend to him now; bid him wait."

The stranger was impatient, and would not be denied.

"Desire him to come in, then," said Matilda.

The domestic hastened to obey her commands.

Verezzi had arisen to leave the room. "No," cried Matilda, "sit still; I shall soon dismiss the fellow; besides, I have no secrets from you." Verezzi took his seat.

The wide folding-doors which led into the passage were open.

Verezzi observed Matilda, as she gazed fixedly through them, to grow pale.

He could not see the cause, as he was seated on a sofa at the other end of the saloon.

Suddenly she started from her seat--her whole frame seemed convulsed by agitation, as she rushed through the door.

Verezzi heard an agitated voice exclaim, "Go! go! to-morrow morning!"

Matilda returned--she seated herself again at the harp which she had quitted, and essayed to compose herself; but it was in vain--she was too much agitated.

Her voice, as she again attempted to sing, refused to perform its office; and her humid hands, as they swept the strings of the harp, violently trembled.

"Matilda," said Verezzi, in a sympathising tone, "what has agitated you? Make me a repository of your sorrows: I would, if possible, alleviate them."

"Oh no," said Matilda, affecting unconcern; "nothing--nothing has happened. I was even myself unconscious that I appeared agitated."

Verezzi affected to believe her, and assumed a composure which he felt not. The conversation changed, and Matilda assumed her wonted mien. The lateness of the hour at last warned them to separate.

The more Verezzi thought upon the evening's occurrence, the more did a conviction in his mind, inexplicable even to himself, strengthen, that Matilda's agitation originated in something of consequence. He knew her mind to be superior to common circumstance and fortuitous casualty, which might have ruffled an inferior soul. Besides, the words which he had heard her utter--"Go! go! to-morrow morning!"--and though he resolved to disguise his real sentiments, and seem to let the subject drop, he determined narrowly to scrutinise Matilda's conduct; and, particularly, to know what took place on the following morning.--An indefinable presentiment that something horrible was about to occur, filled Verezzi's mind. A long chain of retrospection ensued--he could not forget the happy hours which he had passed with Julia; her interesting softness, her ethereal form, pressed on his aching sense.

Still did he feel his soul irresistibly softened towards Matilda--her love for him flattered his vanity; and though he could not feel reciprocal affection towards her, yet her kindness in rescuing him from his former degraded situation, her altered manner towards him, and her unremitting endeavours to please, to humour him in every thing, called for his warmest, his sincerest gratitude.

The morning came--Verezzi arose from a sleepless couch, and descending into the breakfast-parlour, there found Matilda.

He endeavoured to appear the same as usual, but in vain; for an expression of reserve and scrutiny was apparent on his features.

Matilda perceived it, and shrunk abashed from his keen gaze.

The meal passed away in silence.

"Excuse me for an hour or two," at last stammered out Matilda--"my steward has accounts to settle;" and she left the apartment.

Verezzi had now no doubt but that the stranger, who had caused Matilda's agitation the day before, was now returned to finish his business.

He moved towards the door to follow her--he stopped.

What right have I to pry into the secrets of another? thought Verezzi: besides, the business which this stranger has with Matilda cannot possibly concern me.

Still was he compelled, by an irresistible fascination, as it were, to unravel what appeared to him so mysterious an affair. He endeavoured to believe it to be as she affirmed; he endeavoured to compose himself: he took a book, but his eyes wandered insensibly.

Thrice he hesitated--thrice he shut the door of the apartment; till at last, a curiosity, unaccountable even to himself, propelled him to seek Matilda.

Mechanically he moved along the passage. He met one of the domestics--he inquired where Matilda was.

"In the grand saloon," was the reply.

With trembling steps he advanced towards it--The folding-doors were open--He saw Matilda and the stranger standing at the remote end of the apartment.

The stranger's figure, which was towering and majestic, was rendered more peculiarly striking, by the elegantly proportioned form of Matilda, who leant on a marble table near her; and her gestures, as she conversed with him, manifested the most eager impatience, the deepest interest.

At so great a distance, Verezzi could not hear their conversation; but, by the low murmurs which occasionally reached his ear, he perceived that, whatever it might be, they were both equally interested in the subject.

For some time he contemplated them with mingled surprise and curiosity--he tried to arrange the confused murmurs of their voices, which floated along the immense and vaulted apartment, but no articulate sound reached his ear.

At last Matilda took the stranger's hand: she pressed it to her lips with an eager and impassioned gesture, and led him to the opposite door of the saloon.

Suddenly the stranger turned, but as quickly regained his former position, as he retreated through the door; not quickly enough, however, but, in the stranger's fire-darting eye, Verezzi recognised him who had declared eternal enmity at the cottage on the heath.

Scarcely knowing where he was, or what to believe, for a few moments Verezzi stood bewildered, and unable to arrange the confusion of ideas which floated in his brain, and assailed his terror-struck imagination. He knew not what to believe--what phantom it could be that, in the shape of , blasted his straining eye-balls--Could it really be Zastrozzi? Could his most rancorous, his bitterest enemy, be thus beloved, thus confided in, by the perfidious Matilda?

For several moments he stood doubting what he should resolve upon. At one while he determined to reproach Matilda with treachery and baseness, and overwhelm her in the mid career of wickedness; but at last concluding it to be more politic to dissemble and subdue his emotions, he went into the breakfast-parlour which he had left, and seated himself as if nothing had happened, at a drawing which he had left incomplete.

Besides, perhaps Matilda might not be guilty--perhaps she was deceived; and though some scheme of villany and destruction to himself was preparing, she might be the dupe, and not the coadjutor, of . The idea that she was innocent soothed him; for he was anxious to make up, in his own mind, for the injustice which he had been guilty of towards her: and though he could not conquer the disgusting ideas, the unaccountable detestations, which often, in spite of himself, filled his soul towards her, he was willing to overcome what he considered but as an illusion of the imagination, and to pay that just tribute of esteem to her virtues which they demanded.

Whilst these ideas, although confused and unconnected, passed in Verezzi's brain, Matilda again entered the apartment.

Her countenance exhibited the strongest marks of agitation, and full of inexpressible and confused meaning was her dark eye, as she addressed some trifling question to Verezzi, in a hurried accent, and threw herself into a chair beside him.

"Verezzi!" exclaimed Matilda, after a pause equally painful to both--"Verezzi! I am deeply grieved to be the messenger of bad news--willingly would I withhold the fatal truth from you; yet, by some other means, it may meet your unprepared ear. I have something dreadful, shocking, to relate: can you bear the recital?"

The nerveless fingers of Verezzi dropped the pencil--he seized Matilda's hand, and, in accents almost inarticulate from terror, conjured her to explain her horrid surmises.

"Oh! my friend! my sister!" exclaimed Matilda, as well-feigned tears coursed down her cheeks,--"oh! she is--"

"What! what!" interrupted Verezzi, as the idea of something having befallen his adored Julia filled his maddened brain with tenfold horror: for often had Matilda declared, that since she could not become his wife, she would willingly be his friend, and had even called Julia her sister.

"Oh!" exclaimed Matilda, hiding her face in her hands, "Julia--Julia--whom you love, is dead."

Unable to withhold his fleeting faculties from a sudden and chilly horror which seized them, Verezzi sank forward, and, fainting, fell at Matilda's feet.

In vain, for some time, was every effort to recover him. Every restorative which was administered, for a long time, was unavailing: at last his lips unclosed--he seemed to take his breath easier--he moved--he slowly opened his eyes.

Chapter VIII.

His head reposed upon Matilda's bosom; he started from it violently, as if stung by a scorpion, and fell upon the floor. His eyes rolled horribly, and seemed as if starting from their sockets.

"Is she then dead? is Julia dead?" in accents scarcely articulate exclaimed Verezzi. "Ah, Matilda! was it you then who destroyed her? was it by thy jealous hand that she sank to an untimely grave?--Ah, Matilda! Matilda! say that she yet lives! Alas! what have I to do in this world without Julia?--an empty uninteresting void."

Every word uttered by the hapless Verezzi spoke daggers to the agitated Matilda.

Again overpowered by the acuteness of his sensations, he sank on the floor, and, in violent convulsions, he remained bereft of sense.

Matilda again raised him--again laid his throbbing head upon her bosom.-- Again, as recovering, the wretched Verezzi perceived his situation--overcome by agonising reflection, he relapsed into insensibility.

One fit rapidly followed another, and at last, in a state of the wildest delirium, he was conveyed to bed.

Matilda found, that a too eager impatience had carried her too far. She had prepared herself for violent grief, but not for the paroxysms of madness which now seemed really to have seized the brain of the devoted Verezzi.

She sent for a physician--he arrived, and his opinion of Verezzi's danger almost drove the wretched Matilda to desperation.

Exhausted by contending passions, she threw herself on a sofa: she thought of the deeds which she had perpetrated to gain Verezzi's love; she considered that, should her purpose be defeated, at the very instant which her heated imagination had portrayed as the commencement of her triumph; should all the wickedness, all the crimes, into which she had plunged herself, be of no avail-- this idea, more than remorse for her enormities, affected her.

She sat for a time absorbed in a confusion of contending thought: her mind was the scene of anarchy and horror: at last, exhausted by their own violence, a deep, a desperate calm took possession of her faculties. She started from the sofa, and, maddened by the idea of Verezzi's danger, sought his apartment.

On a bed lay Verezzi.

A thick film overspread his eye, and he seemed sunk in insensibility.

Matilda approached him--she pressed her burning lips to his--she took his hand--it was cold, and at intervals slightly agitated by convulsions.

A deep sigh, at this instant, burst from his lips--a momentary hectic flushed his cheek, as the miserable Verezzi attempted to rise.

Matilda, though almost too much agitated to command her emotions, threw herself into a chair behind the curtain, and prepared to watch his movements.

"Julia! Julia!" exclaimed he, starting from the bed, as his flaming eye-balls were unconsciously fixed upon the agitated Matilda, "where art thou? Ah! thy fair form now moulders in the dark sepulchre! would I were laid beside thee! thou art now an ethereal spirit!" and then, in a seemingly triumphant accent, he added, "But, ere long, I will seek thy unspotted soul--ere long I will again clasp my lost Julia!" Overcome by resistless delirium, he was for an instant silent--his starting eyes seemed to follow some form, which imagination had portrayed in vacuity. He dashed his head against the wall, and sank, overpowered by insensibility, on the floor.

Accustomed as she was to scenes of horror, and firm and dauntless as was Matilda's soul, yet this was too much to behold with composure. She rushed towards him, and lifted him from the floor. In a delirium of terror, she wildly called for help. Unconscious of every thing around her, she feared Verezzi had destroyed himself. She clasped him to her bosom, and called on his name, in an ecstasy of terror.

The domestics, alarmed by her exclamations, rushed in. Once again they lifted the insensible Verezzi into the bed--every spark of life seemed now to have been extinguished; for the transport of horror which had torn his soul was almost too much to be sustained. A physician was again sent for--Matilda, maddened by desperation, in accents almost inarticulate from terror, demanded hope or despair from the physician.

He, who was a man of sense, declared his opinion, that Verezzi would speedily recover, though he knew not the event which might take place in the crisis of the disorder, which now rapidly approached.

The remonstrances of those around her were unavailing, to draw Matilda from the bed-side of Verezzi.

She sat there, a prey to disappointed passion, silent, and watching every turn of the hapless Verezzi's countenance, as, bereft of sense, he lay extended on the bed before her.

The animation which was wont to illumine his sparkling eye was fled: the roseate colour which had tinged his cheek had given way to an ashy paleness- he was insensible to all around him. Matilda sat there the whole day, and silently administered medicines to the unconscious Verezzi, as occasion required.

Towards night, the physician again came. Matilda's head thoughtfully leant upon her arm as he entered the apartment.

"Ah, what hope? what hope?" wildly she exclaimed.

The physician calmed her, and bid her not despair: then observing her pallid countenance, he said, he believed she required his skill as much as his patient.

"Oh! heed me not," she exclaimed; "but how is Verezzi? will he live or die?"

The physician advanced towards the emaciated Verezzi--he took his hand.

A burning fever raged through his veins.

"Oh, how is he?" exclaimed Matilda, as, anxiously watching the humane physician's countenance, she thought a shade of sorrow spread itself over his features--"but tell me my fate quickly," continued she: "I am prepared to hear the worst--prepared to hear that he is even dead already."

As she spoke this, a sort of desperate serenity overspread her features--she seized the physician's arm, and looked steadfastly on his countenance, and then, as if overcome by unwonted exertions, she sank fainting at his feet.

The physician raised her, and soon succeeded in recalling her fleeted faculties.

Overcome by its own violence, Matilda's despair became softened, and the words of the physician operated as a balm upon her soul, and bid her feel hope.

She again resumed her seat, and waited with smothered impatience for the event of the decisive crisis, which the physician could now no longer conceal.

She pressed his burning hand in hers, and waited, with apparent composure, for eleven o'clock.

Slowly the hours passed--the clock of Passau tolled each lingering quarter as they rolled away, and hastened towards the appointed time, when the chamberdoor of Verezzi was slowly opened by Ferdinand.

"Ha! why do you disturb me now?" exclaimed Matilda, whom the entrance of Ferdinand had roused from a profound reverie.

"Signora!" whispered Ferdinand--"Signor waits below: he wishes to see you there."

"Ah!" said Matilda thoughtfully, "conduct him here."

Ferdinand departed to obey her--footsteps were heard in the passage, and immediately afterwards stood before Matilda.

"Matilda!" exclaimed he, "why do I see you here? what accident has happened which confines you to this chamber?"

"Ah!" replied Matilda, in an undervoice, "look in that bed--behold Verezzi! emaciated and insensible--in a quarter of an hour, perhaps, all animation will be fled--fled for ever!" continued she, as a deeper expression of despair shaded her beautiful features.

Zastrozzi advanced to the foot of the bed--Verezzi lay, as if dead, before his eyes; for the ashy hue of his lips, and his sunken inexpressive eye, almost declared that his spirit was fled.

Zastrozzi gazed upon him with an indefinable expression of insatiated vengeance--indefinable to Matilda, as she gazed upon the expressive countenance of her coadjutor in crime.

"Matilda! I want you; come to the lower saloon; I have something to speak to you of," said .

"Oh! if it concerned my soul's eternal happiness, I could not now attend," exclaimed Matilda, energetically: "in less than a quarter of an hour, perhaps, all I hold dear on earth will be dead; with him, every hope, every wish, every tie which binds me to earth. Oh!" exclaimed she, her voice assuming a tone of extreme horror, "see how pale he looks!"

Zastrozzi bade Matilda farewell, and went away.

The physician yet continued watching, in silence, the countenance of Verezzi: it still retained its unchanging expression of fixed despair.

Matilda gazed upon it, and waited with the most eager, yet subdued impatience, for the expiration of the few minutes which yet remained--she still gazed.

The features of Verezzi's countenance were slightly convulsed.

The clock struck eleven.

His lips unclosed--Matilda turned pale with terror; yet mute, and absorbed by expectation, remained rooted to her seat.

She raised her eyes, and hope again returned, as she beheld the countenance of the humane physician lighted up with a beam of pleasure.

She could no longer contain herself, but, in an ecstasy of pleasure, as excessive as her grief and horror before had been violent, in rapid and hurried accents questioned the physician. The physician, with an expressive smile, pressed his finger on his lip. She understood the movement; and, though her heart was dilated with sudden and excessive delight, she smothered her joy, as she had before her grief, and gazed with rapturous emotion on the countenance of Verezzi, as, to her expectant eyes, a blush of animation tinged his before-pallid countenance. Matilda took his hand--the pulses yet beat with feverish violence. She gazed upon his countenance--the film, which before had overspread his eye, disappeared: returning expression pervaded its orbit, but it was the expression of deep, of rooted grief.

The physician made a sign to Matilda to withdraw.

She drew the curtain before her, and, in anxious expectation, awaited the event.

A deep, a long-drawn sigh, at last burst from Verezzi's bosom. He raised himself--his eyes seemed to follow some form, which imagination had portrayed in the remote obscurity of the apartment, for the shades of night were but partially dissipated by a lamp which burnt on a table behind. He raised his almost nerveless arm, and passed it across his eyes, as if to convince himself, that what he saw was not an illusion of the imagination. He looked at the physician, who sat near to and silent by the bedside, and patiently awaited whatever event that might occur.

Verezzi slowly arose, and violently exclaimed, "Julia! Julia! my long-lost Julia, come!" And then, more collectedly, he added, in a mournful tone, "Ah no! you are dead; lost, lost for ever!"

He turned round, and saw the physician, but Matilda was still concealed.

"Where am I?" inquired Verezzi, addressing the physician. "Safe, safe," answered he: "compose yourself; all will be well."

"Ah, but Julia?" inquired Verezzi, with a tone so expressive of despair, as threatened returning delirium.

"Oh! compose yourself," said the humane physician: "you have been very ill: this is but an illusion of the imagination; and even now, I fear, that you labour under that delirium which attends a brain-fever."

Verezzi's nerveless frame again sunk upon the bed--still his eyes were open, and fixed upon vacancy: he seemed to be endeavouring to arrange the confusion of ideas which pressed upon his brain.

Matilda undrew the curtain; but, as her eye met the physician's, his glance told her to place it in its original situation.

As she thought of the events of the day her heart was dilated by tumultuous, yet pleasurable emotions. She conjectured, that were Verezzi to recover, of which she now entertained but little doubt, she might easily erase from his heart the boyish passion which before had possessed it; might convince him of the folly of supposing that a first attachment is fated to endure for ever; and, by unremitting assiduity in pleasing him--by soft, quiet attentions, and an affected sensibility, might at last acquire the attainment of that object, for which her bosom had so long and so ardently panted.

Soothed by these ideas, and willing to hear from the physician's mouth a more explicit affirmation of Verezzi's safety than his looks had given, Matilda rose, for the first time since his illness, and, unseen by Verezzi, approached the physician.--"Follow me to the saloon," said Matilda.

The physician obeyed, and, by his fervent assurances of Verezzi's safety and speedy recovery, confirmed Matilda's fluctuating hopes. "But," added the physician, "though my patient will recover if his mind be unruffled, I will not answer for his re-establishment should he see you, as his disorder, being wholly on the mind, may be possibly augmented by--"

The physician paused, and left Matilda to finish the sentence; for he was a man of penetration and judgement, and conjectured that some sudden and violent emotion, of which she was the cause, occasioned his patient's illness. This conjecture became certainty, as, when he concluded, he observed Matilda's face change to an ashy paleness.

"May I not watch him--attend him?" inquired Matilda imploringly.

"No," answered the physician: "in the weakened state in which he now is, the sight of you might cause immediate dissolution."

Matilda started, as if overcome by horror at the bare idea, and promised to obey his commands.

The morning came--Matilda arose from a sleepless couch, and with hopes yet unconfirmed sought Verezzi's apartment.

She stood near the door, listening.--Her heart palpitated with tremulous violence, as she listened to Verezzi's breathing--every sound from within alarmed her. At last she slowly opened the door, and, though adhering to the physician's directions in not suffering Verezzi to see her, she could not deny herself the pleasure of watching him, and busying herself in little offices about his apartment.

She could hear Verezzi question the attendant collectedly, yet as a person who was ignorant where he was, and knew not the events which had immediately preceded his present state.

At last he sank into a deep sleep--Matilda now dared to gaze on him: the hectic colour which had flushed his cheek was fled, but the ashy hue of his lips had given place to a brilliant vermilion--She gazed intently on his countenance.

A heavenly, yet faint smile, diffused itself over his countenance--his hand slightly moved.

Matilda, fearing that he would awake, again concealed herself. She was mistaken; for, on looking again, he still slept.

She still gazed upon his countenance. The visions of his sleep were changed, for tears came fast from under his eyelids, and a deep sigh burst from his bosom.

Thus passed several days: Matilda still watched, with most affectionate assiduity, by the bedside of the unconscious Verezzi.

The physician declared that his patient's mind was yet in too irritable a state to permit him to see Matilda, but that he was convalescent.

One evening she sat by his bedside, and gazing upon the features of the sleeping Verezzi, felt unusual softness take possession of her soul--an indefinable and tumultuous emotion shook her bosom--her whole frame thrilled with rapturous ecstasy, and seizing the hand, which lay motionless beside her, she imprinted on it a thousand burning kisses.

"Ah, Julia! Julia! is it you?" exclaimed Verezzi, as he raised his enfeebled frame; but perceiving his mistake, as he cast his eyes on Matilda, sank back, and fainted.

Matilda hastened with restoratives, and soon succeeded in recalling to life Verezzi's fleeted faculties.

Chapter IX.

Art thou afraid To be the same in thine own act and valour As thou art in desire? would'st thou have that Which thou esteemest the ornament of life. Or live a coward in thine own esteem. Letting I dare not wait upon I would? -- Macbeth.

For love is heaven, and heaven is love. --Lay of the Last Minstrel.

The soul of Verezzi was filled with irresistible disgust, as, recovering, he found himself in Matilda's arms. His whole frame trembled with chilly horror, and he could scarcely withhold himself from again fainting. He fixed his eyes upon the countenance--they met hers--an ardent fire, mingled with a touching softness, filled their orbits.

In a hurried and almost inarticulate accent, he reproached Matilda with perfidy, baseness, and even murder. The roseate colour which had tinged Matilda's cheek, gave place to an ashy hue--the animation which had sparkled in her eye, yielded to a confused expression of apprehension, as the almost delirious Verezzi uttered accusations he knew not the meaning of; for his brain, maddened by the idea of Julia's death, was whirled round in an ecstasy of terror.

Matilda seemed to have composed every passion: a forced serenity overspread her features, as, in a sympathising and tender tone, she entreated him to calm his emotions, and giving him a composing medicine, left him.

She descended to the saloon.

"Ah! he yet despises me--he even hates me," ejaculated Matilda. "An irresistible antipathy--irresistible, I fear, as my love for him is ardent, has taken possession of his soul towards me. Ah! miserable, hapless being that I am! doomed to have my fondest hope, my brightest prospect, blighted."

Alive alike to the tortures of despair and the illusions of hope, Matilda, now in an agony of desperation, impatiently paced the saloon.

Her mind was inflamed by a more violent emotion of hate towards Julia, as she recollected Verezzi's fond expressions: she determined, however, that were Verezzi not to be hers, he should never be Julia's.

Whilst thus she thought, entered

The conversation was concerning Verezzi.

"How shall I gain his love, ?" exclaimed Matilda. "Oh! I will renew every tender office--I will watch by him day and night, and, by unremitting attentions, I will try to soften his flinty soul. But, alas! it was but now that he started from my arms in horror, and, in accents of desperation, accused me of perfidy--of murder. Could I be perfidious to Verezzi, my heart, which burns with so fervent a fire, declares I could not, and murder--"

Matilda paused.

"Would thou could say thou were guilty, or even accessary to that," exclaimed , his eye gleaming with disappointed ferocity. "Would Julia of Strobazzo's heart was reeking on my dagger!"

"Fervently do I join in that wish, my best ," returned Matilda: "but, alas! what avail wishes--what avail useless protestations of revenge, whilst Julia yet lives?--yet lives, perhaps, again to obtain Verezzi--to clasp him constant to her bosom--and perhaps--oh, horror! perhaps to--".

Stung to madness by the picture which her fancy had portrayed, Matilda paused.

Her bosom heaved with throbbing palpitations; and, whilst describing the success of her rival, her warring soul shone apparent from her scintillating eyes.

, meanwhile, stood collected in himself; and scarcely heeding the violence of Matilda, awaited the issue of her speech.

He besought her to calm herself, nor, by those violent emotions, unfit herself for prosecuting the attainment of her fondest hope.

"Are you firm?" inquired .

"Yes!"

"Are you resolved? Does fear, amid the other passions, shake your soul?"

"No, no--this heart knows not to fear--this breast knows not to shrink," exclaimed Matilda eagerly.

"Then be cool--be collected," returned , "and thy purpose is effected."

Though little was in these words which might warrant hope, yet Matilda's susceptible soul, as spoke, thrilled with anticipated delight.

"My maxim, therefore," said , "through life has been, wherever I am, whatever passions shake my inmost soul, at least to appear collected. I generally am; for, by suffering no common events, no fortuitous casualty to disturb me, my soul becomes steeled to more interesting trials. I have a spirit, ardent, impetuous as thine; but acquaintance with the world has induced me to veil it, though it still continues to burn within my bosom. Believe me, I am far from wishing to persuade you from your purpose--No--any purpose undertaken with ardour, and prosecuted with perseverance, must eventually be crowned with success. Love is worthy of any risque--I felt it once, but revenge has now swallowed up every other feeling of my soul--I am alive to nothing but revenge. But even did I desire to persuade you from the purpose on which your heart is fixed, I should not say it was wrong to attempt it; for whatever procures pleasure is right, and consonant to the dignity of man, who was created for no other purpose but to obtain happiness; else, why were passions given us? why were those emotions, which agitate my breast, and madden my brain, implanted in us by nature? As for the confused hope of a future state, why should we debar ourselves of the delights of this, even though purchased by what the misguided multitude calls immorality?"

Thus sophistically argued, .--His soul, deadened by crime, could only entertain confused ideas of immortal happiness; for in proportion as human nature departs from virtue, so far are they also from being able clearly to contemplate the wonderful operations, the mysterious ways of Providence.

Coolly and collectedly argued : he delivered his sentiments with the air of one who was wholly convinced of the truth of the doctrines he uttered,--a conviction to be dissipated by shunning proof.

Whilst thus spoke, Matilda remained silent,--she paused. Zastrozzi must have strong powers of reflection; he must be convinced of the truth of his own reasoning, thought Matilda, as eagerly she yet gazed on his countenance--Its unchanging expression of firmness and conviction still continued.--"Ah!" said Matilda, "Zastrozzi, thy words are a balm to my soul, I never yet knew thy real sentiments on this subject; but answer me, do you believe that the soul decays with the body, or if you do not, when this perishable form mingles with its parent earth, where goes the soul which now actuates its movements? perhaps, it wastes its fervent energies in tasteless apathy, or lingering torments."

"Matilda," returned , "think not so; rather suppose, that by its own inmate and energetical exertions, this soul must endure for ever, that no fortuitous occurrences, no incidental events, can affect its happiness; but by daring boldly, by striving to verge from the beaten path, whilst yet trammelled in the chains of mortality, it will gain superior advantages in a future state."

"But religion! Oh !"--

"I thought thy soul was daring," replied , "I thought thy mind was towering; and did I then err, in the different estimate I had formed of thy character?--O yield not yourself, Matilda thus to false, foolish, and vulgar prejudices--for the present, farewell."

Saying this, departed.

Thus, by an artful appeal to her passions, did extinguish the faint spark of religion which yet gleamed in Matilda's bosom.

In proportion as her belief of an Omnipotent Power, and consequently her hopes of eternal salvation declined, her ardent and unquenchable passion for Verezzi increased, and a delirium of guilty love, filled her soul.--

"Shall I then call him mine for ever?" mentally inquired Matilda; "will the passion which now consumes me, possess my soul to all eternity? Ah! well I know it will; and when emancipated from this terrestrial form, my soul departs; still its fervent energies unrepressed, will remain; and in the union of soul to soul, it will taste celestial transports." An ecstasy of tumultuous and confused delight rushed through her veins: she stood for some time immersed in thought.--Agitated by the emotions of her soul, her every limb trembled--she thought upon 's sentiments, she almost shuddered as she reflected; yet was convinced, by the cool and collected manner in which he had delivered them.--She thought on his advice, and steeling her soul, repressing every emotion, she now acquired that coolness so necessary to the attainment of her desire.

Thinking of nothing else, alive to no idea but Verezzi, Matilda's countenance assumed a placid serenity--she even calmed her soul, she bid it restrain its emotions, and the passions which so lately had battled fiercely in her bosom, were calmed.

She again went to Verezzi's apartment, but, as she approached, vague fears, lest he should have penetrated her schemes confused her: but his mildly beaming eyes, as she gazed upon them, convinced her, that the horrid expressions which he had before uttered, were merely the effect of temporary delirium.

"Ah, Matilda!" exclaimed Verezzi, "where have you been?"

Matilda's soul, alive alike to despair and hope, was filled with momentary delight as he addressed her; but bitter hate, and disappointed love, again tortured her bosom, as he exclaimed in accents of heart-felt agony: "Oh! Julia, my long-lost Julia!"

"Matilda," said he, "my friend, farewell; I feel that I am dying, but I feel pleasure,--oh! transporting pleasure, in the idea that I shall soon meet my Julia. Matilda," added he, "in a softened accent, farewell for ever." Scarcely able to contain the emotions which the idea alone of Verezzi's death excited, Matilda, though the crisis of the disorder, she knew, had been favorable, shuddered--

bitter hate, even more rancorous than ever, kindled in her bosom against Julia, for to hear Verezzi talk of her with soul-subduing tenderness, but wound up her soul to the highest pitch of uncontrollable vengeance.--Her breast heaved violently, her dark eye, in expressive glances, told the fierce passions of her soul; yet, sensible of the necessity of controlling her emotions, she leaned her head upon her hand, and when she answered Verezzi, a calmness, a melting expression of grief, overspread her features. She conjured him in the most tender, the most soothing terms, to compose himself, and, though Julia was gone for ever, to remember that there was yet one in the world, one tender friend who would render the burden of life less insupportable.

"Oh! Matilda," exclaimed Verezzi, "talk not to me of comfort, talk not of happiness, all that constituted my comfort, all to which I looked forward with rapturous anticipation of happiness, is fled--fled for ever."

Ceaselessly did Matilda watch by the bed-side of Verezzi; the melting tenderness of his voice, the melancholy, interesting expression of his countenance, but added fuel to the flame which consumed her: her soul was engrossed by one idea; every extraneous passion was conquered, and nerved for the execution of its fondest purpose; a seeming tranquillity overspread her mind, not that tranquillity which results from conscious innocence, and mild delights, but that which calms every tumultuous emotion for a time; when firm in a settled purpose, the passions but pause, to break out with more resistless violence. In the mean time, the strength of Verezzi's constitution overcame the malignity of his disorder, returning strength again braced his nerves, and he was able to descend to the saloon.

The violent grief of Verezzi had subsided into a deep and settled melancholy; he could now talk of his Julia, indeed it was his constant theme; he spoke of her virtues, her celestial form, her sensibility, and by his ardent professions of eternal fidelity to her memory, unconsciously almost drove Matilda to desperation.--Once he asked Matilda how she died, for on the day when the intelligence first turned his brain, he waited not to hear the particulars, the bare fact drove him to instant madness.

Matilda was startled at the question, yet ready invention supplied the place of a premeditated story.

"Oh! my friend," said she tenderly, "unwillingly do I tell you, that for you she died; disappointed love, like a worm in the bud, destroyed the unhappy Julia; fruitless were all her endeavours to find you, till at last concluding that you were lost to her for ever, a deep melancholy by degrees consumed her, and gently led to the grave--she sank into the arms of death without a groan."

"And there shall I soon follow her," exclaimed Verezzi, as a severer pang of anguish and regret darted through his soul. "I caused her death, whose life was far, far dearer to me than my own. But now it is all over, my hopes of happiness in this world are blasted, blasted for ever."

As he said this, a convulsive sigh heaved his breast, and the tears silently rolled down his cheeks; for some time, in vain were Matilda's endeavours to calm him, till at last, mellowed by time, and overcome by reflection, his violent and fierce sorrow was softened into a fixed melancholy.

Unremittingly Matilda attended him, and gratified his every wish: she, conjecturing that solitude might be detrimental to him, often entertained parties, and endeavoured by gaiety to drive away his dejection, but if Verezzi's spirits were elevated by company and merriment, in solitude again they sank, and a deeper melancholy, a severer regret possessed his bosom, for having allowed himself to be momentarily interested by any thing but the remembrance of his Julia; for he felt a soft, a tender and ecstatic emotion of regret, when retrospection portrayed the blissful time long since gone by, while happy in the society of her whom he idolised, he thought he could be never otherwise than then, enjoying the sweet, the serene delights of association with a congenial mind, he often now amused himself in retracing with his pencil, from memory, scenes which, though in his Julia's society he had beheld unnoticed, yet were now hallowed by the remembrance of her: for he always associated the idea of Julia with the remembrance of those scenes which she had so often admired, and where, accompanied by her, he had so often wandered.

Matilda, meanwhile, firm in the purpose of her soul, unremittingly persevered: she calmed her mind, and though, at intervals, shook by almost super-human emotions, before Verezzi a fixed serenity, a well-feigned sensibility, and a downcast tenderness, marked her manner. Grief, melancholy, a fixed, a quiet depression of spirits, seemed to have calmed every fiercer feeling, when she talked with Verezzi of his lost Julia: but, though subdued for the present, revenge, hate, and the fervour of disappointed love, burned her soul.

Often, when she had retired from Verezzi, when he had talked with tenderness, as he was wont, of Julia, and sworn everlasting fidelity to her memory, would Matilda's soul be tortured by fiercest desperation.

One day, when conversing with him of Julia, she ventured to hint, though remotely, at her own faithful and ardent attachment.

"Think you," replied Verezzi, "that because my Julia's spirit is no longer enshrined in its earthly form, that I am the less devotedly, the less irrevocably hers?--No! no! I was hers, I am hers, and to all eternity shall be hers: and when my soul, divested of mortality, departs into another world, even amid the universal wreck of nature, attracted by congeniality of sentiment, it will seek the unspotted spirit of my idolised Julia.--Oh, Matilda! thy attention, thy kindness, calls for my warmest gratitude--thy virtue demands my sincerest esteem; but, devoted to the memory of Julia, I can love none but her."

Matilda's whole frame trembled with unconquerable emotion, as thus determinedly he rejected her; but, calming the more violent passions, a flood of tears rushed from her eyes; and, as she leant over the back of a sofa on which she reclined, her sobs were audible.

Verezzi's soul was softened towards her--he raised the humbled Matilda, and bid her be comforted, for he was conscious that her tenderness towards him deserved not an unkind return.

"Oh! forgive, forgive me!" exclaimed Matilda, with well-feigned humility; "I knew not what I said."--She then abruptly left the saloon.

Reaching her own apartment, Matilda threw herself on the floor, in an agony of mind too great to be described. Those infuriate passions, restrained as they had been in the presence of Verezzi, now agitated her soul with inconceivable terror. Shook by sudden and irresistible emotions, she gave vent to her despair.

"Where, then, is the boasted mercy of God," exclaimed the frantic Matilda, "if he suffer his creatures to endure agony such as this? or where his wisdom, if he implant in the heart passions furious--uncontrollable--as mine, doomed to destroy their happiness?"

Outraged pride, disappointed love, and infuriate revenge, revelled through her bosom. Revenge, which called for innocent blood--the blood of the hapless Julia.

Her passions were now wound up to the highest pitch of desperation. In indescribable agony of mind, she dashed her head against the floor--she imprecated a thousand curses upon Julia, and swore eternal revenge.

At last, exhausted by their own violence, the warring passions subsided--a calm took possession of her soul--she thought again upon 's advice--Was she now cool? was she now collected?

She was now immersed in a chain of thought; unaccountable, even to herself, was the serenity which had succeeded.

Chapter X.

Persevering in the prosecution of her design, the time passed away slowly to

Matilda; for Verezzi's frame, becoming every day more emaciated, threatened, to her alarmed imagination, approaching dissolution.--Slowly to Verezzi; for he waited with impatience for the arrival of death, since nothing but misery was his in this world.

Useless would it be to enumerate the conflicts in Matilda's soul: suffice it to say, that they were many, and that their violence progressively increased.

Verezzi's illness at last assumed so dangerous an appearance, that Matilda, alarmed, sent for a physician.

The humane man, who had attended Verezzi before, was from home, but one, skilful in his profession, arrived, who declared that a warmer climate could alone restore Verezzi's health.

Matilda proposed to him to remove to a retired and picturesque spot which she possessed in the Venetian territory. Verezzi, expecting speedy dissolution, and conceiving it to be immaterial where he died, consented; and indeed he was unwilling to pain one so kind as Matilda by a refusal.

The following morning was fixed for the journey.

The morning arrived, and Verezzi was lifted into the chariot, being yet extremely weak and emaciated.

Matilda, during the journey, by every care, every kind and sympathising attention, tried to drive away Verezzi's melancholy; sensible that, could the weight which pressed upon his spirits be removed, he would speedily regain health. But, no! it was impossible. Though he was grateful for Matilda's attention, a still deeper shade of melancholy overspread his features; a more heart-felt inanity and languor sapped his life. He was sensible of a total distaste of former objects--objects which, perhaps, had formerly forcibly interested him. The terrific grandeur of the Alps, the dashing cataract, as it foamed beneath their feet, ceased to excite those feelings of awe which formerly they were wont to inspire. The lofty pine-groves inspired no additional melancholy, nor did the blooming valleys of Piedmont, or the odoriferous orangeries which scented the air, gladden his deadened soul.

They travelled on--they soon entered the Venetian territory, where, in a gloomy and remote spot, stood the Castella di Laurentini.

It was situated in a dark forest--lofty mountains around lifted their aspiring and craggy summits to the skies.

The mountains were clothed half up by ancient pines and plane-trees, whose immense branches stretched far; and above, bare granite rocks, on which might be seen, occasionally, a scathed larch, lifted their gigantic and mishapen forms.

In the centre of an amphitheatre, formed by these mountains, surrounded by wood, stood the Castella di Laurentini, whose grey turrets, and time-worn battlements, overtopped the giants of the forest.

Into this gloomy mansion was Verezzi conducted by Matilda. The only sentiment he felt, was surprise at the prolongation of his existence. As he advanced, supported by Matilda and a domestic, into the castella, Matilda's soul, engrossed by one idea, confused by its own unquenchable passions, felt not that ecstatic, that calm and serene delight, only experienced by the innocent, and which is excited by a return to the place where we have spent our days of infancy.

No--she felt not this: the only pleasurable emotion which her return to this remote castella afforded, was the hope that, disengaged from the tumult of, and proximity to the world, she might be the less interrupted in the prosecution of her madly-planned schemes.

Though Verezzi's melancholy seemed rather increased than diminished by the journey, yet his health was visibly improved by the progressive change of air and variation of scenery, which must, at times, momentarily alleviate the most deep-rooted grief; yet, again in a fixed spot--again left to solitude and his own torturing reflections, Verezzi's mind returned to his lost, his still adored Julia. He thought of her ever; unconsciously he spoke of her; and, by his rapturous exclamations, sometimes almost drove Matilda to desperation.

Several days thus passed away. Matilda's passion, which, mellowed by time, and diverted by the variety of objects, and the hurry of the journey, had relaxed its violence, now, like a stream pent up, burst all bounds.

But one evening, maddened by the tender protestations of eternal fidelity to Julia's memory which Verezzi uttered, her brain was almost turned.

Her tumultuous soul, agitated by contending emotions, flashed from her eyes. Unable to disguise the extreme violence of her sensations, in an ecstasy of despairing love, she rushed from the apartment, where she had left Verezzi, and, unaccompanied, wandered into the forest, to calm her emotions, and concert some better plans of revenge; for, in Verezzi's presence, she scarcely dared to think.

Her infuriated soul burned with fiercest revenge: she wandered into the trackless forest, and, conscious that she was unobserved, gave vent to her feelings in wild exclamations.

"Oh! Julia! hated Julia! words are not able to express my detestation of thee. Thou hast destroyed Verezzi--thy cursed image, revelling in his heart, has blasted my happiness for ever; but, ere I die, I will taste revenge--oh! exquisite revenge!" She paused--she thought of the passion which consumed her-- "Perhaps one no less violent has induced Julia to rival me," said she. Again the idea of Verezzi's illness--perhaps his death--infuriated her soul. Pity, chased away by vengeance and disappointed passion, fled.--"Did I say that I pitied thee? Detested Julia, much did my words belie the feelings of my soul. No-- no--thou shalt not escape me.--Pity thee!"

Again immersed in corroding thought, she heeded not the hour, till looking up, she saw the shades of night were gaining fast upon the earth. The evening was calm and serene: gently agitated by the evening zephyr, the lofty pines sighed mournfully. Far to the west appeared the evening star, which faintly glittered in the twilight. The scene was solemnly calm, but not in unison with Matilda's soul. Softest, most melancholy music, seemed to float upon the southern gale. Matilda listened--it was the nuns at a convent, chanting the requiem for the soul of a departed sister.

"Perhaps gone to heaven!" exclaimed Matilda, as, affected by the contrast, her guilty soul trembled. A chain of horrible racking thoughts pressed upon her soul; and, unable to bear the acuteness of her sensations, she hastily returned to the castella.

Thus, marked only by the varying paroxysms of the passions which consumed her, Matilda passed the time: her brain was confused, her mind agitated by the ill success of her schemes, and her spirits, once so light and buoyant, were now depressed by disappointed hope.

What shall I next concert? was the mental inquiry of Matilda. Ah! I know not.

She suddenly started--she thought of .

"Oh! that I should have till now forgotten ," exclaimed Matilda, as a new ray of hope darted through her soul. "But he is now at Naples, and some time must necessarily elapse before I can see him.

"Oh, , Zastrozzi! would that you were here!"

No sooner had she well arranged her resolutions, which before had been confused by eagerness, than she summoned Ferdinand, on whose fidelity she dared to depend, and bid him speed to Naples, and bear a letter, with which he was intrusted, to .

Meanwhile Verezzi's health, as the physician had predicted, was so much improved by the warm climate and pure air of the Castella di Laurentini, that, though yet extremely weak and emaciated, he was able, as the weather was fine, and the summer evenings tranquil, to wander, accompanied by Matilda, through the surrounding scenery.

In this gloomy solitude, where, except the occasional and infrequent visits of a father confessor, nothing occurred to disturb the uniform tenour of their life, Verezzi was every thing to Matilda--she thought of him ever: at night, in dreams, his image was present to her enraptured imagination. She was uneasy, except in his presence; and her soul, shook by contending paroxysms of the passion which consumed her, was transported by unutterable ecstasies of delirious and maddening love.

Her taste for music was exquisite; her voice of celestial sweetness; and her skill, as she drew sounds of soul-touching melody from the harp, enraptured the mind to melancholy pleasure.

The affecting expression of her voice, mellowed as it was by the tenderness which at times stole over her soul, softened Verezzi's listening ear to ecstasy.

Yet, again recovering from the temporary delight which her seductive blandishments had excited, he thought of Julia. As he remembered her ethereal form, her retiring modesty, and unaffected sweetness, a more violent, a deeper pang of regret and sorrow assailed his bosom, for having suffered himself to be even momentarily interested by Matilda.

Hours, days, passed lingering away. They walked in the evenings around the environs of the castella--woods, dark and gloomy, stretched far--cloud-capt mountains reared their gigantic summits high; and, dashing amidst the jutting rocks, foaming cataracts, with sudden and impetuous course, sought the valley below.

Amid this scenery the wily Matilda usually led her victim.

One evening when the moon, rising over the gigantic outline of the mountain, silvered the far-seen cataract, Matilda and Verezzi sought the forest.

For a time neither spoke: the silence was uninterrupted, save by Matilda's sighs, which declared that violent and repressed emotions tortured the bosom within.

They silently advanced into the forest. The azure sky was spangled with stars--not a wind agitated the unruffled air--not a cloud obscured the brilliant concavity of heaven. They ascended an eminence, clothed with towering wood; the trees around formed an amphitheatre. Beneath, by a gentle ascent, an opening showed an immense extent of forest, dimly seen by the moon, which overhung the opposite mountain. The craggy heights beyond might distinctly be seen, edged by the beams of the silver moon.

Verezzi threw himself on the turf.

"What a beautiful scene, Matilda!" he exclaimed.

"Beautiful indeed," returned Matilda. "I have admired it ever, and brought you here this evening on purpose to discover whether you thought of the works of nature as I do."

"Oh! fervently do I admire this," exclaimed Verezzi, as, engrossed by the scene before him, he gazed enraptured.

"Suffer me to retire for a few minutes," said Matilda.

Without waiting for Verezzi's answer, she hastily entered a small tuft of trees. Verezzi gazed surprised; and soon sounds of such ravishing melody stole upon the evening breeze, that Verezzi thought some spirit of the solitude had made audible to mortal ears ethereal music.

He still listened--it seemed to die away--and again a louder, a more rapturous swell, succeeded.

The music was in unison with the scene--it was in unison with Verezzi's soul: and the success of Matilda's artifice, in this respect, exceeded her most sanguine expectation.

He still listened--the music ceased--and Matilda's symmetrical form emerging from the wood, roused Verezzi from his vision.

He gazed on her--her loveliness and grace struck forcibly upon his senses: her sensibility, her admiration of objects which enchanted him, flattered him; and her judicious arrangement of the music, left no doubt in his mind but that, experiencing the same sensations herself, the feelings of his soul were not unknown to her.

Thus far every thing went on as Matilda desired. To touch his feeling had been her constant aim: could she find any thing which interested him; any thing to divert his melancholy; or could she succeed in effacing another from his mind, she had no doubt but that he would quickly and voluntarily clasp her to his bosom.

By affecting to coincide with him in every thing--by feigning to possess that congeniality of sentiment and union of idea, which he thought so necessary to the existence of love, she doubted not soon to accomplish her purpose.

But sympathy and congeniality of sentiment, however necessary to that love which calms every fierce emotion, fills the soul with a melting tenderness, and, without disturbing it, continually possesses the soul, was by no means consonant to the ferocious emotions, the unconquerable and ardent passion which revelled through Matilda's every vein.

When enjoying the society of him she loved, calm delight, unruffled serenity, possessed not her soul. No--but, inattentive to every object but him, even her proximity to him agitated her with almost uncontrollable emotion.

Whilst watching his look, her pulse beat with unwonted violence, her breast palpitated, and, unconscious of it herself, an ardent and voluptuous fire darted from her eyes.

Her passion too, controlled as it was in the presence of Verezzi, agitated her soul with progressively-increasing fervour. Nursed by solitude, and wound up, perhaps, beyond any pitch which another's soul might be capable of, it sometimes almost maddened her.

Still, surprised at her own forbearance, yet strongly perceiving the necessity of it, she spoke not again of her passion to Verezzi.

Chapter XI.

At last the day arrived when Matilda expected Ferdinand's return. Punctual to his time Ferdinand returned, and told Matilda that had, for the present, taken up his abode at a cottage, not far from thence, and that he there awaited her arrival.

Matilda was much surprised that preferred a cottage to her castella; but dismissing that from her mind, hastily prepared to attend him.

She soon arrived at the cottage. met her--he quickened his pace towards her.

"Well, ," exclaimed Matilda, inquiringly.

"Oh!" said , "our schemes have all, as yet, been unsuccessful. Julia yet lives, and, surrounded by wealth and power, yet defies our vengeance. I was planning her destruction, when, obedient to your commands, I came here."

"Alas!" exclaimed Matilda, "I fear it must be ever thus: but, , much I need your advice--your assistance. Long have I languished in hopeless love: often have I expected, and as often have my eager expectations been blighted by disappointment."

A deep sigh of impatience burst from Matilda's bosom, as, unable to utter more, she ceased.

"'Tis but the image of that accursed Julia," replied , "revelling in his breast, which prevents him from becoming instantly yours. Could you but efface that!'"

"I would I could efface it," said Matilda: "the friendship which now exists between us, would quickly ripen into love, and I should be for ever happy. How, , can that be done? But, before we think of happiness, we must have a care to our safety: we must destroy Julia, who yet endeavours, by every means, to know the event of Verezzi's destiny. But, surrounded by wealth and power as she is, how can that be done? No bravo in Naples dare attempt her life: no rewards, however great, could tempt the most abandoned of men to brave instant destruction, in destroying her; and should we attempt it, the most horrible tortures of the Inquisition, a disgraceful death, and that without the completion of our desire, would be the consequence."

"Think not so, Matilda," answered Zastrezzi; "think not, because Julia possesses wealth, that she is less assailable by the dagger of one eager for revenge as I am; or that, because she lives in splendor at Naples, that a poisoned chalice, prepared by your hand, the hand of a disappointed rival, could not send her writhing and convulsed to the grave. No, no; she can die, nor shall we writhe on the rack."

"Oh!" interrupted Matilda, "I care not, if, writhing in the prisons of the Inquisition, I suffer the most excruciating torment; I care not if, exposed to public view, I suffer the most ignominious and disgraceful of deaths, if, before I die--if, before this spirit seeks another world, I gain my purposed design, I enjoy unutterable, and, as yet, inconceivable happiness."

The evening meanwhile came on, and, warned by the lateness of the hour to separate, Matilda and parted.

Zastrozzi pursued his way to the cottage, and Matilda, deeply musing, retraced her steps to the castella.

The wind was fresh, and rather tempestuous: light fleeting clouds were driven rapidly across the dark-blue sky. The moon, in silver majesty, hung high in eastern ether, and rendered transparent as a celestial spirit the shadowy clouds which at intervals crossed her orbit, and by degrees vanished like a vision in the obscurity of distant air. On this scene gazed Matilda--a train of confused thought took possession of her soul--her crimes, her past life, rose in array to her terror-struck imagination. Still burning love, unrepressed, unconquerable passion, revelled through every vein: her senses, rendered delirious by guilty desire, were whirled around in an inexpressible ecstasy of anticipated delight-- delight, not unmixed by confused apprehensions.

She stood thus with her arms folded, as if contemplating the spangled concavity of heaven.

It was late--later than the usual hour of return, and Verezzi had gone out to meet Matilda.

"What! deep in thought, Matilda?" exclaimed Verezzi, playfully.

Matilda's cheek, as he thus spoke, was tinged with a momentary blush; it however quickly passed away; and she replied, "I was enjoying the serenity of the evening, the beauty of the setting sun, and then the congenial twilight induced me to wander farther than usual."

The unsuspicious Verezzi observed nothing peculiar in the manner of Matilda; but, observing that the night air was chill, conducted her back to the castella. No art was left untried, no blandishment omitted, on the part of Matilda, to secure her victim. Every thing which he liked, she affected to admire: every sentiment uttered by Verezzi was always anticipated by the observing Matilda; but long was all in vain--long was every effort to obtain his love useless.

Often, when she touched the harp, and drew sounds of enchanting melody from its strings, whilst her almost celestial form bent over it, did Verezzi gaze enraptured, and, forgetful of every thing else, yielding himself to a tumultuous oblivion of pleasure, listened entranced.

But all her art could not draw Julia from his memory: he was much softened towards Matilda; he felt esteem, tenderest esteem--but he yet loved not.

Thus passed the time.--Often would desperation, and an idea that Verezzi would never love her, agitate Matilda with most violent agony. The beauties of nature which surrounded the eastella had no longer power to interest: borne away on swelling thought, often, in the solitude of her own apartment, her spirit was wafted on the wings of anticipating fancy. Sometimes imagination portrayed the most horrible images for futurity: Verezzi's hate, perhaps his total dereliction of her; his union with Julia, pressed upon her brain, and almost drove her to distraction, for Verezzi alone filled every thought; nourished by restless reveries, the most horrible anticipations blasted the blooming Matilda.--Sometimes, however, a gleam of sense shot across her soul: deceived by visions of unreal bliss, she acquired new courage, and fresh anticipations of delight, from a beam which soon withdrew its ray; for, usually sunk in gloom, her dejected eyes were fixed on the ground; though sometimes an ardent expression, kindled by the anticipation of gratified desire, flashed from their fiery orbits.

Often, whilst thus agitated by contending emotions, her soul was shook, and, unconscious of its intentions, knew not the most preferable plan to pursue, would she seek : on him, unconscious why, she relied much--his words were those of calm reflection and experience; and his sophistry, whilst it convinced her that a superior being exists not, who can control our actions, brought peace to her mind--peace to be succeeded by horrible and resistless conviction of the falsehood of her coadjutor's arguments: still, however, they calmed her; and, by addressing her reason and passions at the same time, deprived her of the power of being benefited by either.

The health of Verezzi, meanwhile, slowly mended: his mind, however, shook by so violent a trial as it had undergone, recovered not its vigour, but, mellowed by time, his grief, violent and irresistible as it had been at first, now became a fixed melancholy, which spread itself over his features, was apparent in every action, and, by resistance, inflamed Matilda's passion to tenfold fury.

The touching tenderness of Verezzi's voice, the dejected softened expression of his eye, touched her soul with tumultuous yet milder emotions. In his presence she felt calmed; and those passions which, in solitude, were almost too fierce for endurance, when with him were softened into a tender though confused delight.

It was one evening, when no previous appointment existed between Matilda and , that, overcome by disappointed passion, Matilda sought the forest.

The sky was unusually obscured, the sun had sunk beneath the western mountain, and its departing ray tinged the heavy clouds with a red glare.--The rising blast sighed through the towering pines, which rose loftily above Matilda's head: the distant thunder, hoarse as the murmurs of the grove, in indistinct echoes mingled with the hollow breeze; the scintillating lightning flashed incessantly across her path, as Matilda, heeding not the storm, advanced along the trackless forest.

The crashing thunder now rattled madly above, the lightnings flashed a larger curve, and at intervals, through the surrounding gloom, showed a scathed larch, which, blasted by frequent storms, reared its bare head on a height above.

Matilda sat upon a fragment of jutting granite, and contemplated the storm which raged around her. The portentous calm, which at intervals occurred amid the reverberating thunder, portentous of a more violent tempest, resembled the serenity which spread itself over Matilda's mind--a serenity only to be succeeded by a fiercer paroxysm of passion.

Chapter XII.

Still sat Matilda upon the rock--she still contemplated the tempest which raged around her.

The battling elements paused: an uninterrupted silence, deep, dreadful as the silence of the tomb, succeeded. Matilda heard a noise--footsteps were distinguishable, and looking up, a flash of vivid lightning disclosed to her view the towering form of .

His gigantic figure was again involved in pitchy darkness, as the momentary lightning receded. A peal of crashing thunder again madly rattled over the zenith, and a scintillating flash announced 's approach, as he stood before Matilda.

Matilda, surprised at his approach, started as he addressed her, and felt an indescribable awe, when she reflected on the wonderful casualty which, in this terrific and tempestuous hour, had led them to the same spot.

"Doubtless his feelings are violent and irresistible as mine: perhaps these led him to meet me here."

She shuddered as she reflected; but smothering the sensations of alarm which she had suffered herself to be surprised by, she asked him what had led him to the forest.

"The same which led you here, Matilda," returned : "the same influence which actuates us both, has doubtless inspired that congeniality which, in this frightful storm, led us to the same spot."

"Oh!" exclaimed Matilda, "how shall I touch the obdurate Verezzi's soul? he still despises me--he declares himself to be devoted to the memory of his Julia;

and that although she be dead, he is not the less devotedly hers. What can be done?"

Matilda paused; and, much agitated, awaited 's reply.

, meanwhile, stood collected in himself, and firm as the rocky mountain which lifts its summit to heaven.

"Matilda," said he, "to-morrow evening will pave the way for that happiness which your soul has so long panted for, if, indeed, the event which will then occur does not completely conquer Verezzi. But the violence of the tempest increases--let us seek shelter."

"Oh! heed not the tempest," said Matilda, whose expectations were raised to the extreme of impatience by 's dark hints--"heed not the tempest, but proceed, if you wish not to see me expiring at your feet."

"You fear not the tumultuous elements--nor do I," replied --"I assert again, that if to-morrow evening you lead Verezzi to this spot--if, in the event which will here occur, you display that presence of mind, which I believe you to possess, Verezzi is yours."

"Ah! what do you say, , that Verezzi will be mine?" inquired Matilda, as the anticipation of inconceivable happiness dilated her soul with sudden and excessive delight.

"I say again, Matilda," returned , "that if you dare to brave the dagger's point--if you but make Verezzi owe his life to you--"

Zastrozzi paused, and Matilda acknowledged her insight of his plan, which her enraptured fancy represented as the basis of her happiness.

"Could he, after she had, at the risk of her own life, saved his, unfeelingly reject her? Would those noble sentiments, which the greatest misfortunes were unable to extinguish, suffer that?--No."

Full of these ideas, her brain confused by the ecstatic anticipation of happiness which pressed upon it, Matilda retraced her footsteps towards the castella.

The violence of the storm which so lately had raged was passed--the thunder, in low and indistinct echoes, now sounded through the chain of rocky mountains, which stretched far to the north--the azure, and almost cloudless either, was studded with countless stars, as Matilda entered the castella, and, as the hour was late, sought her own apartment.

Sleep fled not, as usual, from her pillow; but, overcome by excessive drowsiness, she soon sank to rest.

Confused dreams floated in her imagination, in which she sometimes supposed that she had gained Verezzi; at others, that, snatched from her ardent embrace, he was carried by an invisible power over rocky mountains, or immense and untravelled heaths, and that, in vainly attempting to follow him, she had lost herself in the trackless desert.

Awakened from disturbed and unconnected dreams, she arose.

The most tumultuous emotions of rapturous exultation filled her soul as she gazed upon her victim, who was sitting at a window which overlooked the waving forest.

Matilda seated herself by him, and most enchanting, most pensive music, drawn by her fingers from a harp, thrilled his soul with an ecstasy of melancholy; tears rolled rapidly down his cheeks; deep drawn, though gentle sighs heaved his bosom: his innocent eyes were mildly fixed upon Matilda, and beamed with compassion for one, whose only wish was gratification of her own inordinate desires, and destruction to his opening prospects of happiness.

She, with a ferocious pleasure, contemplated her victim; yet, curbing the passions of her soul, a meekness, a wellfeigned sensibility, characterised her downcast eye.

She waited, with the smothered impatience of expectation, for the evening: then, had affirmed, that she would lay a firm foundation for her happiness.

Unappalled, she resolved to brave the dagger's point: she resolved to bleed; and though her life-blood were to issue at the wound, to dare the event.

The evening at last arrived: the atmosphere was obscured by vapour, and the air more chill than usual; yet, yielding to the solicitations of Matilda, Verezzi accompanied her to the forest.

Matilda's bosom thrilled with inconceivable happiness, as she advanced towards the spot: her limbs, trembling with ecstasy, almost refused to support her. Unwonted sensations--sensations she had never felt before, agitated her bosom; yet, steeling her soul, and persuading herself that celestial transports would be the reward of firmness, she fearlessly advanced.

The towering pine-trees waved in the squally wind--the shades of twilight gained fast on the dusky forest--the wind died away, and a deep, a gloomy silence reigned.

They now had arrived at the spot which had asserted would be the scene of an event which might lay the foundation of Matilda's happiness.

She was agitated by such violent emotions, that her every limb trembled, and Verezzi tenderly asked the reason of her alarm.

"Oh! nothing, nothing!" returned Matilda; but, stung by more certain anticipation of ecstasy by his tender inquiry, her whole frame trembled with tenfold agitation, and her bosom was filled with more unconquerable transport.

On the right, the thick umbrage of the forest trees, rendered undistinguishable any one who might lurk there; on the left, a frightful precipice yawned, at whose base a deafening cataract dashed with tumultuous violence; around, mishapen and enormous masses of rock; and beyond, a gigantic and blackened mountain, reared its craggy summit to the skies.

They advanced towards the precipice. Matilda stood upon the dizzy height-- her senses almost failed her, and she caught the branch of an enormous pine which impended over the abyss.

"How frightful a depth!" exclaimed Matilda.

"Frightful indeed," said Verezzi, as thoughtfully he contemplated the terrific depth beneath.

They stood for some time gazing on the scene in silence.

Footsteps were heard--Matilda's bosom thrilled with mixed sensations of delight and apprehension, as, summoning all her fortitude, she turned round.-- A man advanced towards them.

"What is your business?" exclaimed Verezzi.

"Revenge!" returned the villain, as, raising a dagger high, he essayed to plunge it in Verezzi's bosom, but Matilda lifted her arm, and the dagger piercing it, touched not Verezzi. Starting forward, he fell to the earth, and the ruffian instantly dashed into the thick forest.

Matilda's snowy arm was tinged with purple gore: the wound was painful, but an expression of triumph flashed from her eyes, and excessive pleasure dilated her bosom: the blood streamed fast from her arm, and tinged the rock whereon they stood with a purple stain.

Verezzi started from the ground, and seeing the blood which streamed down Matilda's garments, in accents of terror demanded where she was wounded.

"Oh! think not upon that," she exclaimed, "but tell me--ah! tell me," said she, in a voice of well-feigned alarm, "are you wounded mortally? Oh! what sensations of terror shook me, when I thought that the dagger's point, after having pierced my arm, had drunk your life-blood."

"Oh!" answered Verezzi, "I am not wounded; but let us haste to the castella."

He then tore part of his vest, and with it bound Matilda's arm. Slowly they proceeded towards the castella.

"What villain, Verezzi," said Matilda, "envious of my happiness, attempted his life, for whom I would ten thousand times sacrifice my own? Oh! Verezzi, how I thank God, who averted the fatal dagger from thy heart!"

Verezzi answered not; but his heart, his feelings, were irresistibly touched by Matilda's behaviour. Such noble contempt of danger, so ardent a passion, as to risk her life to preserve his, filled his breast with a tenderness towards her; and he felt that he could now deny her nothing, not even the sacrifice of the poor remains of his happiness, should she demand it.

Matilds's breast meanwhile swelled with sensations of unutterable delight: her soul, borne on the pinions of anticipated happiness, flashed in triumphant glances from her fiery eyes. She could scarcely forbear clasping Verezzi in her arms, and claiming him as her own; but prudence, and a fear of in what manner a premature declaration of love might be received, prevented her.

They arrived at the castella, and a surgeon from the neighbouring convent was sent for by Verezzi.

The surgeon soon arrived, examined Matilda's arm, and declared that no unpleasant consequences could ensue.--Retired to her own apartment, those transports, which before had been allayed by Verezzi's presence, now, unrestrained by reason, involved Matilda's senses in an ecstasy of pleasure.

She threw herself on the bed, and, in all the exaggerated colours of imagination, portrayed the transports which 's artifice has opened to her view.

Visions of unreal bless floated during the whole night in her disordered fancy: her senses were whirled around in alternate ecstasies of happiness and despair, as almost palpable dreams pressed upon her disturbed brain.

At one time she imagined that Verezzi, consenting to their union, presented her his hand: that at her touch the flesh crumbled from it, and, a shrieking spectre, he fled from her view: again, silvery clouds floated across her sight, and unconnected, disturbed visions occupied her imagination till the morning.

Verezzi's manner, as he met Matilda the following morning, was unusually soft and tender; and in a voice of solicitude, he inquired concerning her health.

The roseate flush of animation which tinged her cheek, the triumphant glance of animation which danced in her scintillating eye, seemed to render the inquiry unnecessary.

A dewy moisture filled her eyes, as she gazed with an expression of tumultuous, yet repressed rapture, upon the hapless Verezzi.

Still did she purpose, in order to make her triumph more certain, to protract the hour of victory; and, leaving her victim, wandered into the forest to seek . When she arrived at the cottage, she learnt that he had walked forth.--She soon met him.

"Oh! --my best Zastrozzi!" exclaimed Matilda, "what a source of delight have you opened to me! Verezzi is mine--oh! transporting thought! will be mine for ever. That distant manner which he usually affected towards me, is changed to a sweet, an ecstatic expression of tenderness. Oh! Zastrozzi, receive my best, my most fervent thanks."

"Julia need not die then," muttered ; "when once you possess Verezzi, her destruction is of little consequence."

The most horrible scheme of revenge at this instant glanced across 's mind.

"Oh! Julia must die," said Matilda, "or I shall never be safe; such an influence does her image possess over Verezzi's mind, that I am convinced, were he to know that she lived, an estrangement from me would be the consequence. Oh! quickly let me hear that she is dead. I can never enjoy uninterrupted happiness until her dissolution."

"What you have just pronounced is Julia's death-warrant," said , as he disappeared among the thick trees.

Matilda returned to the castella.

Verezzi, at her return, expressed a tender apprehension, lest, thus wounded, she should have hurt herself by walking; but Matilda quieted his fears, and engaged him in interesting conversation, which seemed not to have for its object the seduction of his affection; though the ideas conveyed by her expressions were so artfully connected with it, and addressed themselves so forcibly to Verezzi's feelings, that he was convinced he ought to love Matilda, though he felt that within himself, which, in spite of reason--in spite of reflection--told him that it was impossible.

Chapter XIII.

The enticing smile, the modest-seeming eye. Beneath whose beauteous beams, belying heaven. Lurk searchless cunning, cruelty, and death. -- Thomson.

Still did Matilda's blandishments--her unremitting attention--inspire Verezzi with a softened tenderness towards her.--He regarded her as one who, at the risk of her own life, had saved his; who loved him with an ardent affection, and whose affection was likely to be lasting: and though he could not regard her with that enthusiastic tenderness with which he even yet adored the memory of his Julia, yet he might esteem her--faithfully esteem her--and felt not that horror at uniting himself with her as formerly. But a conversation which he had with Julia recurred to his mind: he remembered well, that when they had talked of their speedy marriage, she had expressed an idea, that a union in this life might endure to all eternity; and that the chosen of his heart on earth, might, by congeniality of sentiment, be united in heaven.

The idea was hallowed by the remembrance of his Julia; but chasing it, as an unreal vision, from his mind, again his high sentiments of gratitude prevailed.

Lost in these ideas, involved in a train of thought, and unconscious where his footsteps led him, he quitted the castella. His reverie was interrupted by low murmurs, which seemed to float on the silence of the forest: it was scarcely audible, yet Verezzi felt an undefinable wish to know what it was. He advanced towards it--it was Matilda's voice.

Verezzi approached nearer, and from within heard her voice in complaints.-- He eagerly listened.--Her sobs rendered the words, which in passionate exclamations burst from Matilda's lips, almost inaudible. He still listened--a pause in the tempest of grief which shook Matilda's soul seemed to have taken place.

"Oh! Verezzi--cruel, unfeeling Verezzi!" exclaimed Matilda, as a fierce paroxysm of passion seized her brain--"will you thus suffer one who adores you, to linger in hopeless love, and witness the excruciating agony of one who idolises you, as I do, to madness?"

As she spoke thus, a long-drawn sigh closed the sentence.

Verezzi's mind was agitated by various emotions as he stood; but rushing in at last, raised Matilda in his arms, and tenderly attempted to comfort her.

She started as he entered--she heeded not his words; but, seemingly overcome by shame, cast herself at his feet, and hid her face in his robe.

He tenderly raised her, and his expressions convinced her, that the reward of all her anxiety was now about to be reaped.

The most triumphant anticipation of transports to come filled her bosom; yet, knowing it to be necessary to dissemble--knowing that a shameless claim on his affections would but disgust Verezzi, she said--

"Oh! Verezzi, forgive me: supposing myself to be alone--supposing no one overheard the avowal of the secret of my soul, with which, believe me, I never more intended to have importuned you, what shameless sentiments--shameless even in solitude--have I not given vent to. I can no longer conceal, that the passion with which I adore you is unconquerable, irresistible: but, I conjure you, think not upon what you have this moment heard to my disadvantage; nor despise a weak unhappy creature, who feels it impossible to overcome the fatal passion which consumes her.

"Never more will I give vent, even in solitude, to my love--never more shall the importunities of the hapless Matilda reach your ears. To conquer a passion fervent, tender as mine, is impossible."

As she thus spoke, Matilda, seemingly overcome by shame, sank upon the turf.

A sentiment stronger than gratitude, more ardent than esteem, and more tender than admiration, softened Verezzi's heart as he raised Matilda. Her symmetrical from shone with tenfold loveliness to his heated fancy: inspired with sudden fondness, he cast himself at her feet.

A Lethean torpor crept upon his senses; and, as he lay prostrate before

Matilda, a total forgetfulness of every former event of his life swam in his dizzy brain. In passionate exclamations he avowed unbounded love.

"Oh, Matilda! dearest, angelic Matilda!" exclaimed Verezzi, "I am even now unconscious what blinded me--what kept me from acknowledging my adoration of thee!--adoration never to be changed by circumstances--never effaced by time."

The fire of voluptuous, of maddening love, scorched his veins, as he caught the transported Matilda in his arms, and, in accents almost inarticulate with passion, swore eternal fidelity.

"And accept my oath of everlasting allegiance to thee, adored Verezzi," exclaimed Matilda: "accept my vows of eternal, indissoluble love."

Verezzi's whole frame was agitated by unwonted and ardent emotions. He called Matilda his wife--in the delirium of sudden fondness he clasped her to his bosom--"and though love like ours," exclaimed the infatuated Verezzi, "wants not the vain ties of human laws, yet, that our love may want not any sanction which could possibly be given to it, let immediate orders be given for the celebration of our union."

Matilda exultingly consented: never had she experienced sensations of delight like these: the feelings of her soul flushed in exulting glances from her fiery eyes. Fierce, transporting triumph filled her soul as she gazed on her victim, whose mildly-beaming eyes were now characterised by a voluptuous expression. Her heart beat high with transport; and, as they entered the castella, the swelling emotions of her bosom were too tumultuous for utterance.

Wild with passion, she clasped Verezzi to her beating breast; and, overcome by an ecstasy of delirious passion, her senses were whirled around in confused and inexpressible delight. A new and fierce passion raged likewise in Verezzi's breast: he returned her embrace with ardour, and clasped her in fierce transports.

But the adoration with which he now regarded Matilda, was a different sentiment from that chaste and mild emotion which had characterised his love for Julia: that passion, which he had fondly supposed would end but with his existence, was effaced by the arts of another.

Now was Matilda's purpose attained--the next day would behold her his bride--the next day would behold her fondest purpose accomplished.

With the most eager impatience, the fiercest anticipation of transport, did she wait for its arrival.

Slowly passed the day, and slowly did the clock toll each lingering hour as it rolled away.

The following morning at last arrived: Matilda arose from a sleepless couch-- fierce, transporting triumph, flashed from her eyes as she embraced her victim. He returned it--he called her his dear and ever-beloved spouse; and, in all the transports of maddening love, declared his impatience for the arrival of the monk who was to unite them. Every blandishment--every thing which might dispel reflection, was this day put in practice by Matilda.

The monk at last arrived: the fatal ceremony--fatal to the peace of Verezzi-- was performed.

A magnificent feast had been previously arranged; every luxurious viand, every expensive wine, which might contribute to heighten Matilda's triumph, was present in profusion.

Matilda's joy, her soul-felt triumph, was too great for utterance--too great for concealment. The exultation of her inmost soul flashed in expressive glances from her scintillating eyes, expressive of joy intense--unutterable.

Animated with excessive delight, she started from the table, and, seizing

Verezzi's hand, in a transport of inconceivable bliss, dragged him in wild sport and varied movements, to the sound of swelling and soul-touching melody.

"Come, my Matilda," at last exclaimed Verezzi, "come, I am weary of transport--sick with excess of unutterable pleasure: let us retire, and retrace in dreams the pleasures of the day."

Little did Verezzi think that this day was the basis of his future misery: little did he think that, amid the roses of successful and licensed voluptuousness, regret, horror, and despair would arise, to blast the prospects which, Julia being forgot, appeared so fair, so ecstatic.

The morning came.--Inconceivable emotions--inconceivable to those who have never felt them--dilated Matilda's soul with an ecstasy of inexpressible bliss: every barrier to her passion was thrown down--every opposition conquered; still was her bosom the scene of fierce and contending passions.

Though in possession of every thing which her fancy had portrayed with such excessive delight, she was far from feeling that innocent and clam pleasure which soothes the soul, and, calming each violent emotion, fills it with a serene happiness. No--her brain was whirled around in transports; fierce, confused transports of visionary and unreal bliss: though her every pulse, her every nerve, panted with the delight of gratified and expectant desire; still was she not happy; she enjoyed not that tranquillity which is necessary to the existence of happiness.

In this temper of mind, for a short period she left Verezzi, as she had appointed a meeting with her coadjutor in wickedness.

She soon met him.

"I need not ask," exclaimed , "for well do I see, in those triumphant glances, that Verezzi is thine; that the plan which we concerted when last we met, has put you in possession of that which your soul panted for."

"Oh! !" said Matilda,--"kind, excellent Zastrozzi; what words can express the gratitude which I feel towards you--what words can express the bliss exquisite, celestial, which I owe to your advice; yet still, amid the roses of successful love--amid the ecstasies of transporting voluptuousness--fear, blighting chilly fear, damps my hopes of happiness. Julia, the hated, accursed Julia's image, is the phantom which scares my otherwise certain confidence of eternal delight: could she but be hurled to destruction--could some other artifice of my friend sweep her from the number of the living--"

"'Tis enough, Matilda," interrupted ; "'tis enough: in six days hence meet me here; meanwhile, let not any corroding anticipations destroy your present happiness: fear not; but, on the arrival of your faithful Zastrozzi, expect the earnest of the happiness which you wish to enjoy for ever."

Thus saying, departed, and Matilda retraced her steps to her castella.

Amid the delight, the ecstasy, for which her soul had so long panted--amid the embraces of him whom she had fondly supposed alone to constitute all terrestrial happiness, racking, corroding thoughts possessed Matilda's bosom.

Deeply musing on schemes of future delight--delight established by the gratification of most diabolical revenge, her eyes fixed upon the ground, heedless what path she pursued, Matilda advanced along the forest.

A voice aroused her from her reverie--it was Verezzi's--the well-known, the tenderly-adored tone, struck upon her senses forcibly: she started, and, hastening towards him, soon allayed those fears which her absence had excited in the fond heart of her spouse, and on which account he had anxiously quitted the castella to search for her.

Joy, rapturous, ecstatic happiness, untainted by fear, unpolluted by reflection, reigned for six days in Matilda's bosom.

Five days passed away, the sixth arrived, and, when the evening came, Matilda, with eager and impatient steps, sought the forest.

The evening was gloomy, dense vapours overspread the air; the wind, low and hollow, sighed mournfully in the gigantic pine trees, and whispered in low hissings among the withered shrubs which grew on the rocky prominences.

Matilda waited impatiently for the arrival of . At last his towering form emerged from an interstice in the rocks.

He advanced towards her.

"Success! Victory! my Matilda," exclaimed , in an accent of exultation-- "Julia is--"

"You need add no more," interrupted Matilda: "kind, excellent , I thank thee; but yet do say how you destroyed her--tell me by what racking, horrible torments, you launched her soul into eternity. Did she perish by the dagger's point? or did the torments of poison send her, writhing in agony, to the tomb."

"Yes," replied ; "she fell at my feet, overpowered by resistless convulsions. Who more ready than myself to restore the Marchesa's fleeted senses--who more ready than myself to account for her fainting, by observing, that the heat of the assembly had momentarily overpowered her. But Julia's senses were fled for ever; and it was not until the swiftest gondola in Venice had borne me far towards your castella, that il consiglio di dieci searched for, without discovering the offender.

"Here I must remain; for, were I discovered, the fatal consequences to us both are obvious. Farewell for the present," added he, "meanwhile happiness attend you; but go not to Venice."

"Where have you been so late, my love?" tenderly inquired Verezzi as she returned. "I fear lest the night air, particularly that of so damp an evening as this, might affect your health."

"No, no, my dearest Verezzi, it has not," hesitatingly answered Matilda.

"You seem pensive, you seem melancholy, my Matilda," said Verezzi: "lay open your heart to me. I am afraid something, of which I am ignorant, presses upon your bosom.

"Is it the solitude of this remote castella which represses the natural gaiety of your soul? Shall we go to Venice?"

"Oh! no, no!" hastily and eagerly interrupted Matilda: "not to Venice--we must not go to Venice."

Verezzi was slightly surprised, but imputing her manner to indisposition, it passed off.

Unmarked by events of importance, a month passed away. Matilda's passion, unallayed by satiety, unconquered by time, still raged with its former fierceness--still was every earthly delight centred in Verezzi; and, in the air-drawn visions of her imagination, she portrayed to herself that this happiness would last for ever.

It was one evening that Verezzi and Matilda sat, happy in the society of each other, that a servant entering, presented the latter with a sealed paper.

The contents were: "Matilda Contessa di Laurentini is summoned to appear before the holy inquisition--to appear before its tribunal, immediately on the receipt of this summons."

Matilda's cheek, as she read it, was blanched with terror. The summons--the fatal, irresistible summons, struck her with chilly awe. She attempted to thrust it into her bosom; but, unable to conceal her terror, she essayed to rush from the apartment--but it was in vain: her trembling limbs refused to support her, and she sank fainting on the floor.

Verezzi raised her--he restored her fleeting senses; he cast himself at her feet, and in the tenderest, most pathetic accents, demanded the reason of her alarm. "And if," said he, "it is any thing of which I have unconsciously been guilty--if it is any thing in my conduct which has offended you, oh! how soon, how truly would I repent. Dearest Matilda, I adore you to madness: tell me then quickly--confide in one who loves you as I do."

"Rise, Verezzi," exclaimed Matilda, in a tone expressive of serene horror: "and since the truth can no longer be concealed, peruse that letter."

She presented him the fatal summons. He eagerly snatched it: breathless with impatience, he opened it. But what words can express the consternation of the affrighted Verezzi, as the summons, mysterious and inexplicable to him, pressed upon his straining eye-ball. For an instant he stood fixed in mute and agonising thought. At last, in the forced serenity of despair, he demanded what was to be done.

Matilda answered not; for her soul, borne on the pinions of anticipation, at that instant portrayed to itself ignominious and agonising dissolution.

"What is to be done?" again, in a deeper tone of despair, demanded Verezzi.

"We must instantly to Venice," returned Matilda, collecting her scattered faculties: "we must to Venice; there, I believe, we may be safe. But in some remote corner of the city we must for the present fix our habitations: we must condescend to curtail our establishment; and, above all, we must avoid particularity. But will my Verezzi descend from the rank of life in which his birth has placed him, and with the outcast Matilda's fortunes quit grandeur?"

"Matilda! dearest Matilda!" exclaimed Verezzi, "talk not thus; you know I am ever yours; you know I love you, and with you, could conceive a cottage elysium."

Matilda's eyes flushed with momentary triumph as Verezzi spoke thus, amid the alarming danger which impended her: under the displeasure of the inquisition, whose motives for prosecution are inscrutable, whose decrees are without appeal, her soul, in the possession of all it held dear on earth, secure of Verezzi's affection, thrilled with pleasurable emotions, yet not unmixed with alarm.

She now prepared to depart. Taking, therefore, out of all her domestics, but the faithful Ferdinand, Matilda, accompanied by Verezzi, although the evening was far advanced, threw herself into a chariot, and leaving every one at the castella unacquainted with her intentions, took the road through the forest which led to Venice.

The convent bell, almost inaudible from distance, tolled ten as the carriage slowly ascended a steep which rose before it.

"But how do you suppose, my Matilda," said Verezzi, "that it will be possible for us to evade the scrutiny of the inquisition?"

"Oh!" returned Matilda, "we must not appear in our true characters--we must disguise them."

"But," inquired Verezzi, "what crime do you suppose the inquisition to allege against you?"

"Heresy, I suppose," said Matilda. "You know, an enemy has nothing to do but lay an accusation of heresy against any unfortunate and innocent individual, and the victim expires in horrible tortures, or lingers the wretched remnant of his life in dark and solitary cells."

A convulsive sigh heaved Verezzi's bosom.

"And is that then to be my Matilda's destiny?" he exclaimed in horror. "No--

Heaven will never permit such excellence to suffer."

Meanwhile they had arrived at the Brenta. The Brenta's stream glided silently beneath the midnight breeze towards the Adriatic.

Towering poplars, which loftily raised their spiral forms on its bank, cast a gloomier shade upon the placid wave.

Matilda and Verezzi entered a gondola, and the grey tints of approaching morn had streaked the eastern ether, before they entered the grand canal at Venice; and passing the Rialto, proceeded onwards to a small, though not inelegant mansion, in the eastern suburbs.

Every thing here, though not grand, was commodious; and as they entered it, Verezzi expressed his approbation of living here retired.

Seemingly secure from the scrutiny of the inquisition, Matilda and Verezzi passed some days of uninterrupted happiness.

At last, one evening Verezzi, tired even with monotony of ecstasy, proposed to Matilda to take the gondola, and go to a festival which was to be celebrated at St. Mark's Place.

Chapter XIV.

The evening was serene.--Fleecy clouds floated on the horizon--the moon's full orb, in cloudless majesty, hung high in air, and was reflected in silver brilliancy by every wave of the Adriatic, as, gently agitated by the evening breeze, they dashed against innumerable gondolas which crowded the Laguna.

Exquisite harmony, borne on the pinions of the tranquil air, floated in varying murmurs: it sometimes died away, and then again swelling louder, in melodious undulations softened to pleasure every listening ear.

Every eye which gazed on the fairy scene beamed with pleasure; unrepressed gaiety filled every heart but Julia's, as with a vacant stare, unmoved by feelings of pleasure, unagitated by the gaiety which filled every other soul, she contemplated the varied scene. A magnificent gondola carried the Marchesa di Strobazzo; and the innumerable flambeaux which blazed around her rivalled the meridian sun.

It was the pensive, melancholy Julia, who, immersed in thought, sat unconscious of every external object, whom the fierce glance of Matilda measured with a haughty expression of surprise and revenge. The dark fire which flashed from her eye, more than told the feelings of her soul, as she fixed it on her rival; and had it possessed the power of the basilisk's, Julia would have expired on the spot.

It was the ethereal form of the now forgotten Julia which first caught Verezzi's eye. For an instant he gazed with surprise upon her symmetrical figure, and was about to point her out to Matilda, when, in the downcast countenance of the enchanting female, he recognised his long-lost Julia.

To paint the feelings of Verezzi--as Julia raised her head from the attitude in which it was fixed, and disclosed to his view that countenance which he had formerly gazed on in ecstasy, the index of that soul to which he had sworn everlasting fidelity--is impossible.

The Lethean torpor, as it were, which before had benumbed him; the charm, which had united him to Matilda, was dissolved.

All the air-built visions of delight, which had but a moment before floated in gay variety in his enraptured imagination, faded away, and, in place of these, regret, horror, and despairing repentance, reared their heads amid the roses of momentary voluptuousness.

He still gazed entranced, but Julia's gondola, indistinct from distance, mocked his straining eyeball.

For a time neither spoke: the gondola rapidly passed onwards, but, immersed in thought, Matilda and Verezzi heeded not its rapidity.

They had arrived at St. Mark's Place, and the gondolier's voice, as he announced it, was the first interruption of the silence.

They started.--Verezzi now, for the first time, aroused from his reverie of horror, saw that the scene before him was real; and that the oaths of fidelity which he had so often and so fervently sworn to Julia were broken.

The extreme of horror seized his brain--a frigorific torpidity of despair chilled every sense, and his eyes, fixedly, gazed on vacancy.

"Oh! return--instantly return!" impatiently replied Matilda to the question of the gondolier.

The gondolier, surprised, obeyed her, and they returned.

The spacious canal was crowded with gondolas; merriment and splendour reigned around, enchanting harmony stole over the scene; but, listless of the music, heeding not the splendour, Matilda sat lost in a maze of thought.

Fiercest vengeance revelled through her bosom, and, in her own mind, she resolved a horrible purpose.

Meanwhile, the hour was late, the moon had gained the zenith, and poured her beams vertically on the unruffled Adriatic, when the gondola stopped before Matilda's mansion.

A sumptuous supper had been prepared for their return. Silently Matilda entered--silently Verezzi followed.

Without speaking, Matilda seated herself at the supper table: Verezzi, with an air of listlessness, threw himself into a chair beside her.

For a time neither spoke.

"You are not well to-night," at last stammered out Verezzi: "what has disturbed you?"

"Disturbed me!" repeated Matilda: "why do you suppose that any thing has disturbed me?"

A more violent paroxysm of horror seemed now to seize Verezzi's brain. He pressed his hand to his burning forehead--the agony of his mind was too great to be concealed--Julia's form, as he had last seen her, floated in his fancy, and, overpowered by the resistlessly horrible ideas which pressed upon them, his senses failed him: he faintly uttered Julia's name--he sank forward, and his throbbing temples reclined on the table.

"Arise! awake! prostrate, perjured Verezzi, awake!" exclaimed the infuriate Matilda, in a tone of gloomy horror.

Verezzi started up, and gazed with surprise upon the countenance of Matilda, which, convulsed by passion, flashed desperation and revenge.

"'Tis plain," said Matilda, gloomily, "'tis plain, he loves me not."

A confusion of contending emotions battled in Verezzi's bosom: his marriage vow--his faith plighted to Matilda--convulsed his soul with indescribable agony.

Still did she possess a great empire over his soul--still was her frown terrible--and still did the hapless Verezzi tremble at the tones of her voice, as, in a phrensy of desperate passion, she bade him quit her for ever: "And," added she, "go, disclose the retreat of the outcast Matilda to her enemies; deliver me to the inquisition, that a union with her you detest may fetter you no longer."

Exhausted by breathless agitation, Matilda ceased: the passions of her soul flashed from her eyes; ten thousand conflicting emotions battled in Verezzi's bosom; he knew scarce what to do; but, yielding to the impulse of the moment, he cast himself at Matilda's feet, and groaned deeply.

At last the words, "I am ever yours, I ever shall be yours," escaped his lips.

For a time Matilda stood immoveable. At last she looked on Verezzi; she gazed downwards upon his majestic and youthful figure; she looked upon his soul-illumined countenance, and tenfold love assailed her softened soul. She raised him--in an oblivious delirium of sudden fondness she clasped him to her bosom, and, in wild and hurried expressions, asserted her right to his love.

Her breast palpitated with fiercest emotions; she pressed her burning lips to his; most fervent, most voluptuous sensations of ecstasy revelled through her bosom.

Verezzi caught the infection; in an instant of oblivion, every oath of fidelity which he had sworn to another, like a baseless cloud, dissolved away; a Lethean torpor crept over his senses; he forgot Julia, or remembered her only as an uncertain vision, which floated before his fancy more as an ideal being of another world, whom he might hereafter adore there, than as an enchanting and congenial female, to whom his oaths of eternal fidelity had been given.

Overcome by unutterable transports of returning bliss, she started from his embrace--she seized his hand--her face was overspread with a heightened colour as she pressed it to her lips.

"And are you then mine--mine for ever?" rapturously exclaimed Matilda.

"Oh! I am thine--thine to all eternity," returned the infatuated Verezzi: "no earthly power shall sever us; joined by congeniality of soul, united by a bond to which God himself bore witness."

He again clasped her to his bosom--again, as an earnest of fidelity, imprinted a fervent kiss on her glowing cheek; and, overcome by the violent and resistless emotions of the moment, swore, that nor heaven nor hell should cancel the union which he here solemnly and unequivocally renewed.

Verezzi filled an overflowing goblet.

"Do you love me?" inquired Matilda.

"May the lightning of heaven consume me, if I adore thee not to distraction! may I be plunged in endless torments, if my love for thee, celestial Matilda, endures not for ever!"

Matilda's eyes flashed fiercest triumph; the exultingly delightful feelings of her soul were too much for utterance--she spoke not, but gazed fixedly on Verezzi's countenance.

Chapter XV.

That no compunctious visitings of nature Shake my fell purpose, nor keep peace between The effect and it. Come to my woman's breasts. And take my milk for gall, ye murd'ring ministers. Wherever, in your sightless substances. Ye wait on nature's mischief. --Macbeth.

Verezzi raised the goblet which he had just filled, and exclaimed, in an impassioned tone--

"My adored Matilda! this is to thy happiness--this is to thy every wish; and if I cherish a single thought which centres not in thee, may the most horrible tortures which ever poisoned the peace of man, drive me instantly to distraction. God of heaven! witness thou my oath, and write it in letters never to be erased! Ministering spirits, who watch over the happiness of mortals, attend! for here I swear eternal fidelity, indissoluble, unalterable affection to

Matilda!"

He said--he raised his eyes towards heaven--he gazed upon Matilda. Their eyes met--hers gleamed with a triumphant expression of unbounded love.

Verezzi raised the goblet to his lips--when, lo! on a sudden he dashed it to the ground--his whole frame was shook by horrible convulsions--his glaring eyes, starting from their sockets, rolled wildly around: seized with sudden madness, he drew a dagger from his girdle, and with fellest intent raised it high--

What phantom blasted Verezzi's eyeball! what made the impassioned lover dash a goblet to the ground, which he was about to drain as a pledge of eternal love to the choice of his soul! and why did he, infuriate, who had, but an instant before, imagined Matilda's arms an earthly paradise, attempt to rush unprepared into the presence of his Creator!--It was the mildly-beaming eyes of the lovely but forgotten Julia, which spoke reproaches to the soul of Verezzi--it was her celestial countenance, shaded by dishevelled ringlets, which spoke daggers to the false one; for, when he had raised the goblet to his lips--when, sublimed by the maddening fire of voluptuousness to the height of enthusiastic passion, he swore indissoluble fidelity to another--Julia stood before him!

Madness--fiercest madness--revelled through his brain. He raised the poniard high, but Julia rushed forwards, and, in accents of desperation, in a voice of alarmed tenderness, besought him to spare the dagger from his bosom--it was stained with his life's-blood, which trickled fast from the point to the floor. She raised it on high, and impiously called upon the God of nature to doom her to endless torments, should Julia survive her vengeance.

She advanced towards her victim, who lay bereft of sense on the floor: she shook her rudely, and grasping a handful of her dishevelled hair, raised her from the earth.

"Knowest thou me?" exclaimed Matilda, in frantic passion--"knowest thou the injured Laurentini? Behold this dagger, reeking with my husband's blood--behold that pale corse, in whose now cold breast, thy accursed image revelling, impelled to commit the deed which deprives me of happiness for ever."

Julia's senses, roused by Matilda's violence, returned. She cast her eyes upwards, with a timid expression of apprehension, and beheld the infuriate Matilda convulsed by fiercest passion, and a blood-stained dagger raised aloft, threatening instant death.

"Die! detested wretch," exclaimed Matilda, in a paroxysm of rage, as she violently attempted to bathe the stiletto in the life-blood of her rival; but Julia starting aside, the weapon slightly wounded her neck, and the ensanguined stream stained her alabaster bosom.

She fell on the floor, but suddenly starting up, attempted to escape her bloodthirsty persecutor.

Nerved anew by this futile attempt to escape her vengeance, the ferocious Matilda seized Julia's floating hair, and holding her back with fiend-like strength, stabbed her in a thousand places; and, with exulting pleasure, again and again buried the dagger to the hilt in her body, even after all remains of life were annihilated.

At last the passions of Matilda, exhausted by their own violence, sank into a deadly calm: she threw the dagger violently from her, and contemplated the terrific scene before her with a sullen gaze.

Before her, in the arms of death, lay him on whom her hopes of happiness seemed to have formed so firm a basis.

Before her lay her rival, pierced with innumerable wounds, whose head reclined on Verezzi's bosom, and whose angelic features, even in death, a smile of affection pervaded.

There she herself stood, an isolated guilty being. A fiercer paroxysm of passion now seized her: in an agony of horror, too great to be described, she tore her hair in handfuls--she blasphemed the power who had given her being, and imprecated eternal torments upon the mother who had born her.

"And is it for this," added the ferocious Matilda--"is it for horror, for torments such as these, that He, whom monks call all-merciful, has created me?"

She seized the dagger which lay on the floor.

"Ah! friendly dagger," she exclaimed, in a voice of fiend-like horror, "would that thy blow produced annihilation! with what pleasure then would I clasp thee to my heart!"

She raised it high--she gazed on it--the yet warm blood of the innocent Julia trickled from its point.

The guilty Matilda shrunk at death--she let fall the up-raised dagger--her sou had caught a glimpse of the misery which awaits the wicked hereafter, and, spite of her contempt of religion--spite of her, till now, too firm dependence on the doctrines of atheism, she trembled at futurity; and a voice from within which whispers "thou shalt never die!" spoke daggers to Matilda's soul.

Whilst thus she stood entranced in a delirium of despair, the night wore away, and the domestic who attended her, surprised at the unusual hour to which they had prolonged the banquet, came to announce the lateness of the hour; but opening the door, and perceiving Matilda's garments stained with blood, she started back with affright, without knowing the full extent of horror which the chamber contained, and alarmed the other domestics with an account that Matilda had been stabbed.

In a crowd they all came to the door, but started back in terror when they saw Verezzi and Julia stretched lifeless on the floor.

Summoning fortitude from despair, Matilda loudly called for them to return; but fear and horror overbalanced her commands, and, wild with affright, they all rushed from the chamber, except Ferdinand, who advanced to Matilda, and demanded an explanation.

Matilda gave it, in few and hurried words.

Ferdinand again quitted the apartment, and told the credulous domestics, that an unknown female had surprised Verezzi and Matilda; that she had stabbed Verezzi, and then committed suicide.

The crowd of servants, as in mute terror they listened to Ferdinand's account, entertained not a doubt of the truth.--Again and again they demanded an explanation of the mysterious affair, and employed their wits in conjecturing what might be the cause of it; but the more they conjectured, the more were they puzzled; till at last a clever fellow, named Pietro, who, hating Ferdinand on account of the superior confidence with which his lady treated him, and supposing more to be concealed in this affair than met the ear, gave information to the police, and, before morning, Matilda's dwelling was surrounded by a party of officials belonging to il consiglio di dieci.

Loud shouts rent the air as the officials attempted the entrance. Matilda still was in the apartment where, during the night, so bloody a tragedy had been acted; still in speechless horror was she extended on the sofa, when a loud rap at the door aroused the horror-tranced wretch. She started from the sofa in wildest perturbation, and listened attentively. Again was the noise repeated, and the officials rushed in.

They searched every apartment; at last they entered that in which Matilda, motionless with despair, remained.

Even the stern officials, hardy, unfeeling as they were, started back with momentary horror as they beheld the fair countenance of the murdered Julia;

fair even in death, and her body disfigured with numberless ghastly wounds.

"This cannot be suicide," muttered one, who, by his superior manner, seemed to be their chief, as he raised the fragile form of Julia from the ground, and the blood, scarcely yet cold, trickled from her vestments.

"Put your orders in execution," added he.

Two officials advanced towards Matilda, who, standing apart with seeming tranquillity, awaited their approach.

"What wish you with me?" exclaimed Matilda haughtily.

The officials answered not; but their chief, drawing a paper from his vest, which contained an order for the arrest of Matilda La Contessa di Laurentini, presented it to her.

She turned pale; but, without resistance, obeyed the mandate, and followed the officials in silence to the canal, where a gondola waited, and in a short time she was in the gloomy prisons of il consiglio di dieci.

A little straw was the bed of the haughty Laurentini; a pitcher of water and bread was her sustenance; gloom, horror, and despair pervaded her soul: all the pleasures which she had but yesterday tasted; all the ecstatic blisses which her enthusiastic soul had painted for futurity, like the unreal vision of a dream, faded away; and, confined in a damp and narrow cell, Matilda saw that all her hopes of future delight would end in speedy and ignominious dissolution.

Slow passed the time--slow did the clock at St. Mark's toll the revolving hours as languidly they passed away.

Night came on, and the hour of midnight struck upon Matilda's soul as her death knell.

A noise was heard in the passage which led to the prison.

Matilda raised her head from the wall against which it was reclined, and eagerly listened, as if in expectation of an event which would seal her future fate. She still gazed, when the chains of the entrance were unlocked. The door, as it opened, grated harshly on its hinges, and two officials entered.

"Follow me," was the laconic injunction which greeted her terror-struck ear.

Trembling, Matilda arose: her limbs, stiffened by confinement, almost refused to support her; but collecting fortitude from desperation, she followed the relentless officials in silence.

One of them bore a lamp, whose rays darting in uncertain columns, showed, by strong contrasts of light and shade, the extreme massiness of the passages.

The Gothic frieze above was worked with art; and the corbels, in various and grotesque forms, jutted from the tops of clustered pilasters.

They stopped at a door. Voices were heard from within: their hollow tones filled Matilda's soul with unconquerable tremours. But she summoned all her resolution--she resolved to be collected during the trial; and even, if sentenced to death, to meet her fate with fortitude, that the populace, as they gazed, might not exclaim--"The poor Laurentini dared not to die."

These thoughts were passing in her mind during the delay which was occasioned by the officials conversing with another whom they met there.

At last they ceased--an uninterrupted silence reigned: the immense folding doors were thrown open, and disclosed to Matilda's view a vast and lofty apartment. In the centre, was a table, which a lamp, suspended from the centre, overhung, and where two stern-looking men, habited in black vestments, were seated.

Scattered papers covered the table, with which the two men in black seemed busily employed.

Two officials conducted Matilda to the table where they sat, and, retiring, left her there.

Chapter XVI.

Fear, for their scourge, mean villains have;

Thou art the torturer of the brave.

Marmion.

One of the inquisitors raised his eyes; he put back the papers which he was examining, and in a solemn tone asked her name.

"My name is Matilda; my title La Contessa di Laurentini," haughtily she answered; "nor do I know the motive for that inquiry, except it were to exult over my miseries, which you are, I suppose, no stranger to."

"Waste not your time," exclaimed the inquisitor sternly, "in making idle conjectures upon our conduct; but do you know for what you are summoned here?"

"No," replied Matilda.

"Swear that you know not for what crime you are here imprisoned," said the inquisitor.

Matilda took the oath required. As she spoke, a dewy sweat burst from her brow, and her limbs were convulsed by the extreme of horror, yet the expression of her countenance was changed not.

"What crime have you committed which might subject you to the notice of this tribunal?" demanded he, in a determined tone of voice.

Matilda gave no answer, save a smile of exulting scorn. She fixed her regards upon the inquisitor: her dark eyes flashed fiercely, but she spoke not.

"Answer me," exclaimed he, "what to confess might save both of us needless trouble."

Matilda answered not, but gazed in silence upon the inquisitor's countenance.

He stamped thrice--four officials rushed in, and stood at some distance from Matilda.

"I am unwilling," said the inquisitor, "to treat a female of high birth with indignity; but if you confess not instantly, my duty will not permit me to withhold the question."

A deeper expression of contempt shaded Matilda's beautiful countenance: she frowned, but answered not.

"You will persist in this foolish obstinacy?" exclaimed the inquisitor.-- "Officials, do your duty."

Instantly the four, who till now had stood in the back-ground, rushed forwards: they seized Matilda, and bore her into the obscurity of the apartment.

Her dishevelled ringlets floated in negligent luxuriance over her alabaster bosom: her eyes, the contemptuous glance of which had now given way to a confused expression of alarm, were almost closed; and her symmetrical form, as borne away by the four officials, looked interestingly lovely.

The other inquisitor, who, till now, busied by the papers which lay before him, had heeded not Matilda's examination, raised his eyes, and beholding the form of a female, with a commanding tone of voice, called to the officials to stop.

Submissively they obeyed his order.--Matilda, released from the fell hands of these relentless ministers of justice, advanced to the table.

Her extreme beauty softened the inquisitor who had spoken last. He little thought that, under a form so celestial, so interesting, lurked a heart depraved, vicious as a demon's.

He therefore mildly addressed her; and telling her that, on some future day, her examination would be renewed, committed her to the care of the officials, with orders to conduct her to an apartment better suited to her rank.

The chamber to which she followed the officials was spacious and well furnished, but large iron bars secured the windows, which were high, and impossible to be forced.

Left again to solitude, again to her own gloomy thoughts--her retrospection but horror and despair--her hopes of futurity none--her fears many and horrible--Matilda's situation is better conceived than described.

Floating in wild confusion, the ideas which presented themselves to her imagination were too horrible for endurance.

Deprived, as she was, of all earthly happiness, fierce as had been her passion for Verezzi, the disappointment of which sublimed her brain to the most infuriate delirium of resistless horror, the wretched Matilda still shrunk at death--she shrunk at the punishment of those crimes, in whose perpetration no remorse had touched her soul, for which, even now, she repented not, but as they had deprived her of terrestrial enjoyments.

She thought upon the future state--she thought upon the arguments of against the existence of a Deity: her inmost soul now acknowledged their falsehood, and she shuddered as she reflected that her condition was irretrievable.

Resistless horror revelled through her bosom: in an intensity of racking thought she rapidly paced the apartment; at last, overpowered, she sank upon a sofa.

At last the tumultuous passions, exhausted by their own violence, subsided: the storm, which so lately had agitated Matilda's soul, ceased; a serene calm succeeded, and sleep quickly overcame her faculties.

Confused visions flitted in Matilda's imagination whilst under the influence of sleep; at last they assumed a settled shape.

Strangely brilliant and silvery clouds seemed to flit before her sight: celestial music, enchanting as the harmony of the spheres, serened Matilda's soul, and, for an instant, her situation forgotten, she lay entranced.

On a sudden the music ceased; the azure concavity of heaven seemed to open at the zenith, and a being, whose countenance beamed with unutterable beneficence, descended.

It seemed to be clothed in a transparent robe of flowing silver: its eye scintillated with super-human brilliancy, whilst her dream, imitating reality almost to exactness, caused the entranced Matilda to suppose that it addressed her in these words:--

"Poor sinning Matilda! repent, it is not yet too late.--God's mercy is unbounded.--Repent! and thou mayest yet be saved."

These words yet tingled in Matilda's ears; yet were her eyes lifted to heaven, as if following the visionary phantom who had addressed her in her dream, when, much confused, she arose from the sofa.

A dream so like reality made a strong impression upon Matilda's soul.

The ferocious passions, which so lately had battled fiercely in her bosom, were calmed: she lifted her eyes to heaven: they beamed with an expression of sincerest penitence; for sincerest penitence, at this moment, agonised whilst it calmed Matilda's soul.

"God of mercy! God of heaven!" exclaimed Matilda; "my sins are many and horrible, but I repent."

Matilda knew not how to pray; but God, who from the height of heaven penetrates the inmost thoughts of terrestrial hearts, heard the outcast sinner, as in tears of true and agonising repentance she knelt before him.

She despaired no longer--She confided in the beneficence of her Creator; and, in the hour of adversity, when the firmest heart must tremble at his power, no longer a hardened sinner, demanded mercy. And mercy, by the All-benevolent of heaven, is never refused to those who humbly, yet trusting in his goodness, ask it.

Matilda's soul was filled with a celestial tranquillity. She remained upon her knees in mute and fervent thought: she prayed; and, with trembling, asked forgiveness of her Creator.

No longer did that agony of despair torture her bosom. True, she was ill at ease: remorse for her crimes deeply affected her; and though her hopes of salvation were great, her belief in God and a future state firm, the heavy sighs which burst from her bosom, showed that the arrows of repentance had penetrated deeply.

Several days passed away, during which the conflicting passions of Matilda's soul, conquered by penitence, were mellowed into a fixed and quiet depression.

Chapter XVII.

Si fractus illabatur orbis. Impavidum ferient ruin?--Horace.

At last the day arrived, when, exposed to a public trial, Matilda was conducted to the tribunal of il consiglio di dieci.

The inquisitors were not, as before, at a table in the middle of the apartment; but a sort of throne was raised at one end, on which a stern-looking man, whom she had never seen before, sat: a great number of Venetians were assembled, and lined all sides of the apartment.

Many, in black vestments, were arranged behind the superior's throne; among whom Matilda recognised those who had before examined her.

Conducted by two officials, with a faltering step, a pallid cheek, and downcast eye, Matilda advanced to that part of the chamber where sat the superior.

The dishevelled ringlets of her hair floated unconfined over her shoulders: her symmetrical and elegant form was enveloped in a thin white robe.

The expression of her sparkling eyes was downcast and humble; yet, seemingly unmoved by the scene before her, she remained in silence at the tribunal.

The curiosity and pity of every one, as they gazed on the loveliness of the beautiful culprit, was strongly excited.

"Who is she? who is she?" ran in inquiring whispers round the apartment.-- No one could tell.

Again deep silence reigned--not a whisper interrupted the appalling calm.

At last the superior, in a sternly solemn voice, said--

"Matilda Contessa di Laurentini, you are here arraigned on the murder of La Marchesa di Strobazzo: canst thou deny it? canst thou prove to the contrary? My ears are open to conviction. Does no one speak for the accused?"

He ceased: uninterrupted silence reigned. Again he was about--again, with a look of detestation and horror, he had fixed his penetrating eye upon the trembling Matilda, and had unclosed his mouth to utter the fatal sentence, when his attention was arrested by a man who rushed from the crowd, and exclaimed, in a hurried tone--

"La Contessa di Laurentini is innocent." "Who are you, who dare assert that?" exclaimed the superior, with an air of doubt.

"I am," answered he, "Ferdinand Zeilnitz, a German, the servant of La Contessa di Laurentini, and I dare assert that she is innocent."

"Your proof," exclaimed the superior, with a severe frown.

"It was late," answered Ferdinand, "when I entered the apartment, and then I beheld two bleeding bodies, and La Contessa di Laurentini, who lay bereft of sense on the sofa."

"Stop!" exclaimed the superior.

Ferdinand obeyed.

The superior whispered to one in black vestments, and soon four officials entered, bearing on their shoulders an open coffin.

The superior pointed to the ground: the officials deposited their burden, and produced, to the terror-struck eyes of the gazing multitude, Julia, the lovely Julia, covered with innumerable and ghastly gashes.

All present uttered a cry of terror--all started, shocked and amazed, from the horrible sight; yet some, recovering themselves, gazed at the celestial loveliness of the poor victim to revenge, which, unsubdued by death, still shone from her placid features.

A deep-drawn sigh heaved Matilda's bosom; tears, spite of all her firmness, rushed into her eyes; and she had nearly fainted with dizzy horror; but, overcoming it, and collecting all her fortitude, she advanced towards the corse of her rival, and, in the numerous wounds which covered it, saw the fiat of her future destiny.

She still gazed on it--a deep silence reigned--not one of the spectators, so interested were they, uttered a single word--not a whisper was heard through the spacious apartment.

"Stand off! guilt-stained, relentless woman," at last exclaimed the superior fiercely: "is it not enough that you have persecuted, through life, the wretched female who lies before you--murdered by you? Cease, therefore, to gaze on her with looks as if your vengeance was yet insatiated. But retire, wretch: officials, take her into your custody; meanwhile, bring the other prisoner."

Two officials rushed forward, and led Matilda to some distance from the tribunal; four others entered, leading a man of towering height and majestic figure. The heavy chains with which his legs were bound, rattled as he advanced.

Matilda raised her eyes-- stood before her.

She rushed forwards--the officials stood unmoved.

"Oh, !" she exclaimed--"dreadful, wicked has been the tenour of our life; base, ignominious, will be its termination: unless we repent, fierce, horrible, may be the eternal torments which will rack us, ere four and twenty hours are elapsed. Repent then, Zastrozzi; repent! and as you have been my companion in apostasy to virtue, follow me likewise in dereliction of stubborn and determined wickedness."

This was pronounced in a low and faltering voice.

"Matilda," replied , whilst a smile of contemptuous atheism played over his features--"Matilda, fear not: fate wills us to die: and I intend to meet death, to encounter annihilation, with tranquillity. Am I not convinced of the non-existence of a Deity? am I not convinced that death will but render this soul more free, more unfettered? Why need I then shudder at death? why need any one, whose mind has risen above the shackles of prejudice, the errors of a false and injurious superstition."

Here the superior interposed, and declared he could allow private conversation no longer.

Quitting Matilda, therefore, , unappalled by the awful scene before him, unshaken by the near approach of agonising death, which he now fully believed he was about to suffer, advanced towards the superior's throne.

Every one gazed on the lofty stature of , and admired his dignified mein and dauntless composure, even more than they had the beauty of Matilda.

Every one gazed in silence, and expected that some extraordinary charge would be brought against him.

The name of , pronounced by the superior, had already broken the silence, when the culprit, gazing disdainfully on his judge, told him to be silent, for he would spare him much needless trouble.

"I am a murderer," exclaimed ; "I deny it not: I buried my dagger in the heart of him who injured me; but the motives which led me to be an assassin were at once excellent and meritorious; for I swore, at a loved mother's death-bed, to revenge her betrayer's falsehood.

"Think you, that whilst I perpetrated the deed I feared the punishment? or whilst I revenged a parent's cause, that the futile torments which I am doomed to suffer here, had any weight in my determination? No--no. If the vile deceiver, who brought my spotless mother to a tomb of misery, fell beneath the dagger of one who swore to revenge her--if I sent him to another world, who destroyed the peace of one I loved more than myself in this, am I to be blamed?"

Zastrozzi ceased, and, with an expression of scornful triumph, folded his arms.

"Go on!" exclaimed the superior.

"Go on! go on!" echoed from every part of the immense apartment.

He looked around him. His manner awed the tumultuous multitude; and, in uninterrupted silence, the spectators gazed upon the unappalled , who, towering as a demi-god, stood in the midst.

"Am I then called upon," said he, "to disclose things which bring painful remembrances to my mind? Ah! how painful! But no matter; you shall know the name of him who fell beneath this arm: you shall know him, whose memory, even now, I detest more than I can express. I care not who knows my actions, convinced as I am, and convinced to all eternity as I shall be, of their rectitude.--Know, then, that Olivia was my mother; a woman in whom every virtue, every amiable and excellent quality, I firmly believe to have been centred.

"The father of him who by my arts committed suicide but six days ago in La Contessa di Laurentini's mansion, took advantage of a moment of weakness, and disgraced her who bore me. He swore with the most sacred oaths to marry her--but he was false.

"My mother soon brought me into the world--the seducer married another; and when the destitute Olivia begged a pittance to keep her from starving, her proud betrayer spurned her from his door, and tauntingly bade her exercise her profession.--The crime I committed with thee, perjured one! exclaimed my mother as she left his door, shall be my last!--and, by heavens! she acted nobly. A victim to falsehood, she sank early to the tomb, and, ere her thirtieth year, she died--her spotless soul fled to eternal happiness.--Never shall I forget, though but fourteen when she died--never shall I forget her last commands.-- My son, said she, my Pietrino, revenge my wrongs--revenge them on the perjured Verezzi--revenge them on his progeny for ever.

"And, by heaven! I think I have revenged them. Ere I was twenty-four, the false villain, though surrounded by seemingly impenetrable grandeur; though forgetful of the offence to punish which this arm was nerved, sank beneath my dagger. But I destroyed his body alone," added , with a terrible look of insatiated vengeance: "time has taught me better: his son's soul is hell-doomed to all eternity: he destroyed himself; but my machinations, though unseen, effected his destruction.

"Matilda di Laurentini! Hah! why do you shudder?. When, with repeated stabs, you destroyed her who now lies lifeless before you in her coffin, did you not reflect upon what must be your fate? You have enjoyed him whom you adored--you have even been married to him--and, for the space of more than a month, have tasted unutterable joys, and yet you are unwilling to pay the price of your happiness--by heavens I am not!" added he, bursting into a wild laugh.--"Ah! poor fool, Matilda, did you think it was from friendship I instructed you how to gain Verezzi?--No, no--it was revenge which induced me to enter into your schemes with zeal; which induced me to lead her, whose lifeless form lies yonder, to your house, foreseeing the effect it would have upon the strong passions of your husband.

"And now," added , "I have been candid with you. Judge, pass your sentence--but I know my doom; and, instead of horror, experience some degree of satisfaction at the arrival of death, since all I have to do on earth is completed."

Zastrozzi ceased; and, unappalled, fixed his expressive gaze upon the superior.

Surprised at 's firmness, and shocked at the crimes of which he had made so unequivocal an avowal, the superior turned away in horror.

Still stood unmoved, and fearlessly awaited the fiat of his destiny.

The superior whispered to one in black vestments. Four officials rushed in, and placed on the rack.

Even whilst writhing under the agony of almost insupportable torture his nerves were stretched, 's firmness failed him not; but, upon his soul-illumined countenance, played a smile of most disdainful scorn; and with a wild convulsive laugh of exulting revenge--he died.

THE END

CPSIA information can be obtained
at www.ICGtesting.com
Printed in the USA
LVOW08s0342021116
511207LV00018B/2084/P